C

Critical acclai

'Cranny evol … eeling by writing about … to being literature'
Sunday Sun Times

'A celebration of Irishness'
Yorkshire Post

'Cranny, in his auspicious debut, evokes, with a gentle lyrical touch, the warmth, as well as the wounding pride, the conflicting emotions, the flow of past into present, so often found in Irish family relationships'
Publishers Weekly

Robert Cranny was born in Ireland and emigrated to the United States in 1950 when he was eighteen. He now lives in New York City.

ON US THY POOR CHILDREN

Robert Cranny

A STAR BOOK

published by

the Paperback Division of
W. H. ALLEN & Co. Ltd

A Star Book

Published in 1983
by the Paperback Division of
W. H. Allen & Co. Ltd
A Howard and Wyndham Company
44 Hill Street, London W1X 8LB

First published in the United States of America by
The Dial Press, 1982
First published in Great Britain by
W. H. Allen & Co. Ltd, 1982

Printed in Great Britain by
Cox & Wyman Ltd, Reading

ISBN 0 352 31300 5

FOR MY DAUGHTER,
ADRIENNE

I wish to express my deep gratitude
to William Goyen for helping me
sing out of myself.

Pitiful brother; what frightful nights I owed him; I have not put enough ardor into this enterprise. I have trifled with his infirmity. My fault should we go back to exile and to slavery. He implied I was unlucky and of a very strange innocence, and would add disquieting reasons.

—Rimbaud

ON US
THY POOR CHILDREN

I sat under the tree, hidden, looking across the field, frightened that anyone would see me because I hadn't gone to school. I had pleaded with my mother to keep me home. "But what will you do at home?" she asked me. "In the name of God will you stop breaking my heart and leave me in peace. Sure it can't be as bad as all that." When I left the house I knew I wasn't going to school.

It was a bright November morning, the frost thick on the ground. When I had looked out the bedroom window that morning I thought it had snowed but it was only the frost. The sun shone brightly, and the sky was clear. It was a beautiful morning, but I was frightened. When I turned up toward Sutton's Field I knew I would go over to the Boley Woods. I hoped nobody had seen me. I knew that after nine o'clock nobody would come up through the field and I would be alone.

There was a low stone wall between the field and the woods. I saw the goalposts in the field and I wished that all I had to do was play football for the rest of my life. When I ran across the field, I felt a huge expectation as if some wonderful thing inside me would burst and I knew I could leap high in the air and run and run and I wanted everyone to see me. But now I sat hidden under the tree. Nearly all the leaves were gone and the beechnuts were scattered on the ground.

The nine o'clock whistle from Sutton's Dairy sounded, and I knew everybody would be sitting down at their desks, taking out their Irish books because that's what we had first every morning. I took out my Irish book, too, and somehow I knew that if I was looking at it, it wasn't so bad that I wasn't in school. Off through the trees I could see the long gravel driveway that led up to Sir Valentine Grace's house. I saw him coming down the driveway on his bicycle, and I wondered where he was going and what he did. He didn't have to go to school. He went down the drive and down Sutton's Hill, passing the women on their way to ten o'clock mass. I knew my mother was on her way there, too. They would all be in the church for the mass, where they were given the strength to make their way through the day. Afterward they would go up to the town and shop for the day's dinner. And I knew that my father was in the bakery in Dublin. He was in his singlet and the white trousers and those old boots he wore when he worked, which had no laces, the tongues sticking out of them. "There is nobody works as hard as your father," my mother would say. "They'd have to go a long way to catch up to him."

Some mornings I heard him leave the house. The front gate would shut, the bolt would fall back into place. Then I'd hear his footsteps walking off toward Monkstown to catch the early tram. Sometimes I'd hear him call out a greeting. "Soft morning, John," he would say, and I knew it was Mr. Mooney. Some mornings I could even hear the low hum of the tram away in the distance and I knew he was on it. I knew that later in the day he would walk down through the field on his way home. He would get off the bus at the top of the hill and if he wasn't going to stop at Baker's for a pint he would be home early. My mother would have his dinner ready. He usually didn't eat with us except on Sundays, when we all sat down together. He had his tea brought to him in the living room. He would prop the paper up in front of him to read and lean it back against the milk jug for support. He had lost all his teeth many years before. He had a set of false teeth but only wore them when he went walking. When he ate he took them out and chewed the meat with his gums. "For God's sake why don't you use your teeth?" my mother would say to him. "I never had a tougher piece of meat in my life," he would say back to her. "If the meat was tender I wouldn't have any trouble." "That's the tenderest piece of meat Egan had in the shop. There is nothing wrong with the meat. For God's sake stop complaining about the meat being tough and you without a tooth in your head." He would lift his head from the paper and turn back again as if he were reading. After a silence he would say, "Christ you'd take anything from that auld Egan. You'd take any damn thing at all he gives you. I don't know why you go there at all. I don't know where the hell he gets it. You don't need teeth with a good piece of meat." My mother would raise her eyes to the heavens and go back out to the kitchen and leave him at the table. She would shake her head for a long time and then look at us and start to laugh silently and we would laugh with her. "What's going on out there?" my father would ask.

Then my mother would say, "Are you ready for another cup of tea?" "Yes," he would answer, "and a biscuit, too, if you have it."

There were times when he was so close to us, but at other times so distant. We knew when to stay far from him. On the good days we would watch him at the table. He never left anything on his plate and he insisted on something green every day. "You'll never go wrong if you have something green every day," he said. Sometimes he would beckon us to the table and take a piece of meat on his fork. "Eat this now," he'd say. It always tasted so good from his plate. My mother would say to him, "O Johnny, they have had their own, don't be feeding them." "Oh, it's just a bit," he'd say. "Well it's little enough you have for yourself," she'd tell him. "Eat it yourself now." And then she would tell us to move away from the table. But on the days he stalked silently into the house shooting glances at us as if we were agonies he had to endure, my mother would usher us out of the kitchen and we would go outside or into the living room or upstairs. He'd bring a strange silence into the house with him. We could hear the hall clock tick, and my mother would close the kitchen door. We knew he was sitting darkly over his food just waiting for any small complaint that he could use to set off an outburst. We would start to play and then after a while forget that he was home. In our games we would raise our voices or shout or laugh; then suddenly his terrifying roar would explode. We would tiptoe across the room and sit down. We tried to hide our fear from each other. Paul, who was three years older than me, would stick his tongue out toward the kitchen. I was so frightened; I was sure our father would know he was doing it.

I sat all morning under the beech tree. I changed the books at what I thought were the appropriate times. I didn't take out the math book. I couldn't bear to see it. The English book looked so rich with its lovely red cover. I liked to pick it up and smell it. But the math book had a smell that frightened me.

The world was far away. I couldn't hear it at all but when I looked toward the sky I could see the tops of the houses and I knew it was there. The women were coming back from the town to cook dinner and soon the twelve o'clock bell would be clanging in the schoolyard and all the boys would come streaming home up the Willy Gambols Hill, past Monkstown Castle and then down the road past the field. I decided I would wait until I heard the one o'clock whistle from the dairy before I would come out. Everybody would be home and they wouldn't see me and I would casually make my way home. I hid my schoolbag under a bush and I came out into the field. When I walked into the house I wondered if my mother could tell I hadn't gone to school. I tried to be the same way I was every day when I came home.

"You are late today," she said as I walked in. "What kept you?"

"Oh, I just had to go over some homework," I said.

"Well, you don't have too much time. You shouldn't have to rush your lunch," she said.

"I've plenty of time," I answered. I began to feel sorry I hadn't gone to school because all it did was complicate things. I suddenly found it very hard to eat and I lost my appetite.

"What's the matter with you?" my mother asked.

"Nothing," I said.

"Well, why aren't you eating?"

"I'm eating," I said and it was then that I arrived at my plan for the afternoon. I would ask her for sixpence for a copybook and I would use it to go to the pictures. That was better than sitting under a tree. And I'd collect my schoolbag on the way home. I had a thought for an instant of asking her to let me stay home for the afternoon but I knew she wouldn't relent.

"Come on now," she said. "You'll be late."

"I'll be all right," I said.

"Well, I must say you are very casual today," she said. "I don't know what's gotten into you at all. I'm just waiting for you to ask me to let you stay home, so if you are going to ask me, the answer is no."

"I wasn't going to ask," I said with great indignation.

"No, nor don't," she said quickly. "Hurry up now and get back."

I stood up from the table and started to put on my jacket and then in the most casual way I said, "Could I have sixpence for a copybook?"

"Where now do you think I would get sixpence?" she said to me. "Didn't you just buy a new copybook?"

"It's full," I told her. "Auld Martin is always giving us compositions and he always wants four pages."

She walked over to the mantel and picked up her purse and looked into it. She moved the coins up and down. I knew I was going to get the money. She found a sixpence and she said, "Here, you'll have me in the poorhouse."

I took it from her and quickly left.

It was a strange feeling. Triumph and guilt. I had taken the sixpence and I knew how tight money was. There was never enough. Ah but never mind. Off you go, I told myself, and I made my way down to the Astoria. I thought about my mother on the way. I knew that she worked in the house in Monkstown. My father didn't know about it.

I sat through Hopalong Cassidy and forgot that I shouldn't be there. It was all far far away in another place and in another time. On the way home I hummed to myself and felt that the day had turned out well. All that remained for me now was to make my entrance, complain to all of what a tough day it had been, and then settle in for the evening.

The tea was ready when I arrived home. My sister Mary and my mother were sitting at the kitchen table. My father was in the living room with the evening paper. I had retrieved my schoolbag from under the bushes and I made a cheerful entrance with no trace of guilt.

"Hello," I said as I sat down at the table.

"Well, how are you now?" my mother asked.

"Grand, thanks," I said.

"And would you like a cup of tea?" she asked me as if I were the lord of the manor.

"Please," I said.

"And how did you like the pictures?" she asked as she moved to the stove.

"I wasn't at the pictures," I said.

"Well now, where's the copybook you bought? Is it in your bag? Would you like me to take a look?"

"How did you know I went to the pictures?" I asked.

"Because Eddie Moran knocked at the door a half an hour ago and said that Mr. Martin wanted to know why you weren't at school."

"And what did you tell him?"

"I told him you were doing some messages for me," she said.

That idiot Eddie Moran, I thought.

"And now what do you think of that?" she asked me. "Your mother having to tell lies for you. Isn't that a nice how-do-you-do. Wait till your father hears about this."

"And are you going to tell him?" I asked.

I gave her an imploring look, and she didn't say anything. She poured herself a cup of tea and she put the kettle back on the stove and came back and sat down at the table.

"I've a good mind to tell him," she said. "Telling lies and

spending money I can ill afford. I don't know why you have to behave like that. Why did you tell me lies and take me for a fool?" She looked at me with pain in her face and I wanted to cry. "I don't know what the hell gets into you at all. Can you tell me why you didn't go to school?"

"Because we have math for two hours every Tuesday and I'm no good at it and I never get anything right. I always fail at it," I said. "And Martin always brings me up to the blackboard and he tells me to do the sums and I can never do them and then I always get slapped. Six on each hand he gave me the other day. I'll never be able to do them."

My sister and my mother looked at each other.

"Are you going to tell Dad?" I asked her again.

"You must promise it will never happen again."

"I swear," I answered, "I'll never do it again."

"Well, let me tell you, me bucko, the next time you do anything like that I won't hesitate to tell your father. You're just lucky he wasn't here when Eddie Moran came to the house."

Life could have been wonderful if only there wasn't math. Why was there math? Mr. Martin had brought me up in front of the class one day when we were having Irish. I was the only one in the class who had translated a phrase into Gaelic and when I did it he called me up and held me in front of him with his arms around me and he embraced me. In his lovely Kerry way he said to me and to the class, "Oh, if only you had the arithmetic. What in the name of all that's holy is it?" The class looked up at me, and I could smell his tobacco smell.

When he would take down the big Irish history from the shelf above his desk and read to us, I loved that the best of all. The ancient stories brought a warmth to me that I couldn't understand, and when I spoke Gaelic and heard the words come off my tongue there was a power in them. I loved the way the Gaelic was written in my Irish book. I loved the sound of my name when Mr. Martin called it out in Irish. Every time he read the book I wondered where it had all gone. Where was Tara now? There were always defeats and betrayals and battles nearly won, or the French never came or there was a great storm and the great armada was scattered and lost. The people huddled in ditches and on the sides of the roads and the redcoats ran over the country. There were defeats and more defeats and desolation and sadness. I was always anticipating the next defeat. I had a sorrow inside me that I couldn't express. I was ashamed. I sat helpless in the class and it was all in the book and it never changed.

Our town was a place of large families. The Tullys had sixteen children. "I don't know where they put them all," my mother used to say. "Where in the name of God do they all sleep, and look at Mr. Tully and the cut of the poor children. Not a stitch on them without a patch. Sure God help them, I don't know how he does it. All the time in the pub and the mother such a lovely woman. I'm sure they all go to bed hungry at night. Be thankful for what you have. By God none of you ever went to bed hungry in this house. They can say what they like about your father, none of you were ever left hungry."

Jimmy Tully was in my class, and I used to call for him at his house. He would often have a piece of bread in his hand, and when we walked he would take small bites as if he were trying to make it last. He didn't seem to mind that there were fifteen others besides himself. He was one of the cleverest boys in the class, too, and I always wanted to ask him where they all slept. Mrs. Tully always smiled when I passed her. She had an air about her, elegant and soft even in her shabby clothes. She had all those children and everybody knew that Mr. Tully came home drunk every night. He came up the street on his bicycle weaving from side to side, and then he would pause and just sit astride it with his long legs holding him in place, swaying from side to side as if he were listening to a secret tune. There were times he'd fall asleep on the bicycle and forget to pedal and fall down. He never looked at us. Even in his drunkenness there was that impassive look. He would close his eyes and bow his head and then he would resume his journey home, and Jimmy often came running out of the house to take the bicycle in for him.

"God help the poor Tullys. The poor father, lovely-looking man that he is but sure there are a lot more like him," my mother would often say as she waited for my father to come home. We sat around the fire with her and she knitted and talked to us and she would look at the clock on the mantelpiece. I could hear the steel needles clicking together. I couldn't take my eyes off them. Her hands moved quickly as if they had a life of their own and were not a part of her at all. She could look across the kitchen at something that might catch her eye and her hands went on knitting by themselves.

As the evening grew darker she became anxious, although she tried not to show it. She would glance at the clock. "Your father is late." Sometimes she bit her lip and stared into the fire. If one of us was making too much noise, she would look up and say, "Ah, don't do that." She'd say it kindly, her face red in the glow of the fire, and I'd want my father to come home. I'd get up and go out to the front door and walk down to the gate. Was that him coming down from the field? It was hard to tell in the gloom. Whoever it was, he was staggering. "God, I hope it's him," I would pray and feel relieved when it wasn't, and the man passed on going to some other house. Oh, come home, come home. He could have fallen off the bus. God knows what's happened to him. We were all thinking the same thing but we couldn't say a word of it to each other. And then I would go into the house and when my mother heard the front door open she would think it was him, then see it was only me and say, "Will you stay in or stay out?"

Sometimes she would put her knitting down and hold a book in front of her. Her lips moved as she read and her white hair was wispy over her forehead and she leaned forward in her chair. There was only the gentle whispering of the fire and a slight rumble as it settled in the grate. We all stared into it now as if it held a secret. The fire knew where he was. Our fear was for ourselves. We all hoped he'd come home sober and that my mother wouldn't have to deal with him drunk. "He couldn't be in the city all this time," my mother would say. "He's probably down in the harbor bar. I don't like him being with that York Road crowd. I don't know why he goes there; sure they're only good for drinking his money. Jesus, he doesn't see much of theirs." And then the silence again.

One night we heard the front gate open and clang shut again. We heard the footsteps on the path, the sound of the key turning in the lock and the front door opening. One sound led to the other. The gate, the steps, the key in the door. The door opened, and he strode in smiling at us. He knew what we were thinking, and now there he stood and he was sober. My stomach turned over in relief and I couldn't help smiling. My mother jumped up and made her way to the stove and started his dinner.

"A hard day, Johnny?" she asked him over her shoulder.

"Wasn't bad at all, wasn't bad at all. It wasn't what you'd call the worst. No indeed it wasn't bad at all."

He was mellow. Not drunk at all but mellow and happy to be home. We all looked at him and he winked at us and put his hand into his pocket and pulled out a bag of sweets. He put it down in the middle of the kitchen table. "This is for them that was good today. Were they all good today, Kelly?" he asked my mother.

"Oh, they were not bad at all," she said. "You can all have one each and then finish your homework and up to bed with you."

We protested and said, "But Paul Temple is on tonight."

"Well now, mister," my father said, "you can Paul Temple yourself up to bed."

I looked at my mother. "It's the final episode tonight," I told her. She loved to listen to Paul Temple, too. It was a radio serial about a detective. She never missed him.

"Well all right," she said, "but after that it's up to bed." And we listened. It was warm and cozy in the house and my father was home and it was nice to be eating sweets. We couldn't hear any noise from the outside at all. We were all home sitting in the kitchen.

I was born in the house next door to the McQueens. My sister Mary told me that John Hill's cab took me to the church when I was christened. When the cab started off down the road all the children ran after it. Mary said it was a Sunday, a lovely sunny day, "and you didn't cry even when the priest poured the Holy Water on you." "There wasn't a sound out of him," they told my mother because she couldn't go to the church. "Ah sure he's a grand little fellow," she said. A lot of people came to the house in the afternoon and they all looked at me and sat and talked and had a cup of whiskey if they wanted it or a bottle of porter.

Mary told me one day how I got the name Jackie. "Well, we were all sitting in the living room, and I was standing by my father's chair and Mrs. McQueen came in with Mr. McQueen. Well, she walked over to the crib and looked down at you. 'O Jackie you're gorgeous. O Jackie you must be the most beautiful baby in all of Ireland. O Jackie wait till they walk down the pier with you, you'll be stolen away.' O Jackie, she kept saying. O Jackie this and O Jackie that and by the time the afternoon was over they were all calling you Jackie, Master Jackie. And that's how you got your name."

We moved away from Carysfort Road and the McQueens when I was three. Mrs. McQueen didn't like to see us move. She used to say, "There is no one like your mother. You couldn't ask for a better neighbor. There isn't a gentler creature on God's earth. Oh, I'm terrible fond of your mother." Mrs. McQueen was a Belfast Protestant and Mr. McQueen was a Catholic, but he never went to mass. He had fought in the First World War and been gassed. He had a terrible cough and there were times when he would go into such a spasm of coughing I thought he was going to die. He was a tall, good-looking man with gray hair, and his dog was always at his side. He moved about the house as if he didn't want to be noticed. Mrs. McQueen would shout at him, and he would quietly go up the stairs to the bedroom, and then as if everything was all right she would turn to me. "You were a gorgeous baby," she would say. "I never saw a lovelier head of hair on a child and to this day I've never seen a pair of eyes like yours."

She had a sharp Belfast accent and even when she was mellow her accent made her sound angry. She chewed seaweed because she said there was no better thing for you. The seaweed came in a cellophane bag. I tried it one day. I wanted to spit it out, but I was afraid to, so I swallowed it and told her it was very nice but I didn't want any more.

There was a piano in the living room and Dorry McQueen used to play it. Sometimes she would take my hands in hers and she would move them up and down the keyboard. She would start slowly, then do it faster and faster. She always played "Here comes the man with the mandolin," and everybody used to sing. There were four girls and Dorry was the youngest. They all had boyfriends except her but all the boys were after her. On Sunday afternoons the boyfriends came to the house. There were others, too. They sat in the living room and smoked and talked and when they whispered they'd look at me to see if I heard. Dorry told them she was going to wait for me.

When the boys came to the house Dorry used to change the way she talked. She would put on an accent and pronounce all the words differently. She often brought me up to the bedroom and I watched her get ready. She showed me how she put her lipstick on and asked me if her hair was all right in the back because she combed it up and then she'd ask me if her slip was hanging. When she had put her makeup on she'd look at herself in the long mirror. She looked at her teeth and sometimes she had pimples on her face and she got angry at them and put more makeup on and she'd look in the mirror again and say, "This isn't the right shade. I can't go out like this."

When Davy McQueen came home from England they were always happy and excited. He would play his accordion and they would sing. There was a lot of work in England and they said there was nothing but Irish in Birmingham. Davy was handsome and he looked like his father. All his sisters were crazy about him. "If Davy wasn't my brother I'd marry him," Dorry used to say. She always kissed him before she went out and when Mrs. McQueen looked at him she smiled, too, and all the hardness left her face.

There was one Sunday when Jenny McQueen brought her boyfriend to the house. His name was Joe Dolan and he was a Catholic. Mrs. McQueen didn't like Jenny going out with a Catholic boy, but Joe had been in the Royal Navy and had been wounded. "There has to be something decent in him," Mrs. McQueen said. "He isn't like all the other blackguards. And he has a chance at a good trade, too. Didn't they train him as an electrician?"

It broke her heart though when Davy came home from England and brought his bride with him. Her name was Audrey. He got married in England and didn't tell anyone. He said that they were only going to stay a short while and then they were going to live in England for good.

When I knocked at the door one Sunday Dorry opened it and she hardly smiled at all. "You can't stay too long today," she said. "Davy is leaving and everything is upside down." She pulled me in and I followed her to the living room. Mrs. McQueen was drinking a cup of tea in her chair by the fire and she hardly looked up. "Hello, Jackie," she said very quietly. She was bent forward in the chair and her pale green cardigan was opened and her hair hadn't been combed. She held the cup of tea in her hand and she stared into it. "All the good times are gone," she said. She still looked down into her cup. "Aye indeed, all the good times are gone. You'll be leaving, too, one day. You will," she said, looking over to where I was sitting on the sofa. "That's all this bloody country is good for—leaving."

Dorry moved close to her and put her hand on her shoulder and Mrs. McQueen started to sob.

"What else can he do, Mother?" Dorry said. "What can he do?"

"Oh, he could have found something here. He's not like the others. He doesn't belong with the blackguards." She was silent again for a while and she took out a small lace-edged handkerchief from her pocket and she dabbed gently at her eyes and then looked down into her tea. "Well if he's leaving today they better get up," she said. "Go up and knock at the door," she said to Dorry.

Dorry went up the stairs, and I could hear her knocking on the bedroom door. Mrs. McQueen was bent over in the chair lower than before and she turned her head to me and whispered, "None of them like Audrey at all. Nobody has a good word to say for her. She's not warm. She's just not nice. I don't know what in the name of God he sees in her." There were footsteps on the stairs and she put her finger to her lips and looked down into her cup again.

"They're getting up," Dorry said.

"Well it will be a short day for them here," Mrs. McQueen said. "It's nearly noon now and the boat leaves at six and by the time they have a bit to eat and do their packing it will be time for them to leave. Sure we hardly had a visit at all. And Audrey never left his side."

Mr. McQueen moved quietly into the room and sat in the chair opposite his wife. "Did the papers come yet?" he asked.

"Who bloody cares about the papers?" she said. "Go out and take a look for yourself."

"I was only asking," he said quietly. "I just thought somebody might have brought them in."

"Well you are the only one that reads them," she said to him. "Who the hell else would bring them in?"

"All right, all right," he said softly. "I'll go take a look for myself."

He rose from his chair and went to the front door. I heard it open and then close again and here he came with the papers. "Well, are you satisfied now?" Mrs. McQueen said to him. He didn't answer. He wet his fingers in his mouth and began to turn the pages. He coughed softly and cleared his throat. He coughed again. Then the coughs began to come quickly—he was having a spasm. His head was bent, and his eyes were so wide open I thought they were going to come out of his head. He held the papers on his knees with one hand and he shook and coughed. Mrs. McQueen glanced at him, annoyed, and then closed her eyes. In the middle of the spasm Davy and Audrey came into the room. The coughing went on and on and nobody could say a word until it was over. Finally it subsided and Mr. McQueen calmly went back to his paper.

"Well you don't have much time," Mrs. McQueen said to Davy. She didn't look at Audrey. Then she said, "Will you have breakfast?"

"That would be good," Davy said. He held Audrey's hand and sat back on the couch and smiled at her while Mrs. McQueen hurried to the kitchen. I often saw her in the kitchen among the pots and pans and the crockery. She would look through the kitchen window at the little patch where she grew her vegetables. She would stare through the window and then the tears would come.

While Mrs. McQueen was in the kitchen, Dorry started to play the piano. "Tiddly oom pom pom, tiddly oom pom pom. Here comes the man with the mandolin." She played and she sang and looked at Davy. He smiled at her and he started to sing and Audrey was happy beside him. All the regular Sunday crowd began to arrive and Mrs. McQueen brought the couple their breakfast. She did like the crowd. She heard the music and she saw them all laughing and she began to smile.

The living room was full. You would never think that Davy and his Audrey were going away. He was laughing and talking and Mrs. McQueen sat beside him on a small stool by the edge of the couch and watched him eating. Dorry was still at the piano with a crowd of men around her and the front door kept opening and closing and Joe Dolan and Jenny sat together holding hands.

It could have gone on like that all the time if Davy hadn't decided to go away. Mrs. Quinn wanted him to stay at home. "It's the place where you were brought up and where all the neighbors respect you. Oh, sure Davy they all think the world of you and you could have your pick of what there is to be had," she would say. "And is there any nicer place in the world than right here? With the sea at your feet and the mountains at your back. Oh, I don't understand it all. Why they all have to go away I don't know. They get over there and they get a taste of the other side and something gets into them. What in the name of God is it at all. And did you ever see the like of them when they come back. They are all talk about how much they love to be home and there's no place like it and it's the most beautiful place in the world and then off they go again."

Davy strapped his accordion on and started to play. His fingers moved up and down on the keys and he moved his head from side to side as he played. Mrs. McQueen didn't take her eyes off him. He looked so much like his father.

"The sea at your feet and the mountains at your back are all right for a while. They'll be there for a long time," Davy had said. And if he had looked out the window he could have seen Dalkey Hill looking down over the town. Always looking at them. In ten minutes they could be down in Bullock harbor and in a skiff and be out on the water with the lines cast. The sport they had when the mackerel were running. And was there ever such a sight as the sunset on Killiney Hill?

The music finally stopped and everyone's attention turned to the conversation Davy was having with John Boylan. "Sure there is going to be massive changes in the world," Davy was saying. "All sorts of changes, wait till you see. There has to be. They didn't fight the war to keep things the way they were. Oh, you'll see, all right. Massive changes and all sorts of inventions."

"Sure aren't things all right as they are?" said John Boylan. He was short, with his hair neatly combed to the side. He had a job in the civil service. He was very clever, they said, and there was a great future for him. "Aren't we all right the way we are?" he went on. "What do we want a lot of changes for?"

"Oh, it's well for some people, some people don't have to worry," said Davy. "Some people have cushy jobs and then they wonder what's the matter with the rest of us."

"Ah now, wait a minute, Davy. You can't say that of me. It has nothing to do with my job. Whether I had it or not I'd stay here. I'd knock out a living some way."

"But let's face it, John, there isn't room for a man to grow here. If you have ambition what can you do with it here, tell me that? God, I've seen the brightest chaps walking the streets with their hands in their pockets and not two pennies to rub together. Let me tell you, John, I've seen those same chaps in Birmingham and they run rings around Englishmen when it comes to doing the job. Why shouldn't they go there? What the hell is there for them here? You can't spend all your life sitting up on the Vico Road looking at the lovely view."

Boylan looked sad, and then someone said, "You are right there, Davy. It's no use. We'll always be coming and going and the thing of it is it's nobody's fault. It's just the way it is."

Mrs. McQueen looked at the clock. She turned to Davy

and said it was time to get ready. They all began to stand up and then Joe Tunney said, "Why don't we all go down to the boat with them. What? We'll all go down and give them a proper send-off. We'll do it in style. Wait a minute now. Wait a minute," and then he ran out the door.

Davy and Audrey went upstairs to get ready and everybody was standing with their glasses in their hands, talking softly. It had been a lovely afternoon and they wanted it to go on. They were resigned to comings and goings.

We heard the clip-clip of hooves on the street and when we looked through the window there was Joe Tunney leading a column of horse-drawn cabs to the door. "We are not going to a funeral," someone shouted. He came in to the living room and said, "We will send them off in style. We will have a royal procession down to the harbor where the couple will embark for the land of the pagans across the sea."

"Pagans my arse," said Mrs. McQueen. "There are more pagans in Ireland than in the land across the sea."

"Well, whatever they are, they're bad enough," said Joe Tunney. "Are we right now? Is the couple ready? Are we ready to make our way?"

Davy came down the stairs. The luggage was placed outside and everyone started to move slowly out to the front gate. The jarvies sat on the cabs and there was a crowd of children outside the gate. The neighbors stood watching. "It's only Davy McQueen going away," they said.

They came out of the house and climbed into the cabs and everyone joked and shouted. Mr. McQueen was standing at the gate with the newspaper still in his hand. He looked after them and the paper flapped in the breeze. The dog stood by him. Mrs. McQueen wore her good coat with a lovely scarf around her neck and she looked like a lady. "To the manor born," was what Joe Tunney used to say when he saw her. She put just a touch of lipstick on her lips and she wore her good shoes, too, which made her look as though she had grown a foot taller. She walked very straight, with a regal bearing, taking small, quick steps as she walked down the path to the front gate. Joe Tunney held the door open for her and she got in with Davy and his bride. Dorry was in the cab, too. I sat beside her and then Joe Tunney got in. He stuck his head out the window and shouted, "Are we right? Are we leaving anybody behind?" Davy leaned out and waved to Mr. McQueen still standing at the gate with the paper in his hand. He waved back feebly, murmuring "Good-bye, God bless," and then he coughed a little and cleared his throat and turned and made his way slowly back to the house. The dog followed behind him.

The procession started to move away. The neighbors waved and called good-bye and the children ran down the street after them. "Sure you'd think he was the only one ever left," someone said. Singing came from the other cabs. "I'll take you home again Cathleen," and then "Now is the hour when we must say good-bye, soon we'll be sailing far across the sea."

We turned down to the seafront and past Bullock harbor. It was early evening and the skiffs were still in the water, and the crowds were still sitting on the harbor walls with their lines out. The sea lay calm before them.

Mrs. McQueen looked just at Davy, who sat opposite her. Every once in a while there was a shout from behind or a piece of a song or the sound of laughter but as we came closer to the harbor, it got quieter and we all began to realize Davy and his bride were really leaving. His accordion was in its black case on top of the cab with the rest of his luggage. The harbor and the great granite East Pier lay before us. It was a promenade pier, crowded as it always was on a Sunday. We could hear the faint strains of the band playing.

I could tell the tide was in because the sea covered the mark on the pier. Joe Tunney said it must be a spring tide because the water was even higher than the mark. "Well anyway the boat is in," he said. "You can see the masts over the pier."

"You don't have to go, you know," Mrs. McQueen said, turning to Davy. "You aren't being put out of the house. There's nobody says you have to go. Back and forth to that bloody place. Not me. I wouldn't leave. They couldn't drag me out of here."

Davy leaned over and took her hands and looked into her eyes. "You don't have to, either," he said softly. "What would I have to come back to if you left? Will you tell me that? What would I have to come back to?"

Mrs. McQueen looked down and started to cry softly. She took her handkerchief from her pocket and dabbed at her eyes. She looked beaten. All of a sudden she was old. Her eyes were red and watery like the eyes of an old woman; her wispy gray hair hung limply. There was hardly a trace of her lipstick left, and she shivered. He held her hands as she cried. There was no sound from her, just the tears, and she wiped them away with her handkerchief. Audrey reached over to her and placed her hand on her arm. Mrs. McQueen didn't look at her but only stared down at the floor, her body weaving with the motion of the cab.

We were right by the pier now. The cab stopped, and we could hear the shouts of the others behind us: "All off, all off." The cab doors swung open; the jarvies jumped down, their top hats angled on their heads. "It's a lovely evening for a crossing," one of them said. The seafront was crowded with Sunday strollers and there was a stream of people heading down to the pier with luggage. We got out of the cab and stood while the cabman took the luggage down from the roof. The sky began to cloud over; it began to get dark. Big drops of rain began to fall. "Oh, sure it's only a sun shower," said the jarvey. "Be God they're on you before you know it and look across the road would you. It isn't raining there at all. Ah you could never keep up with the weather. Now that's the thing we have that has England beat. Be Jesus the weather. I never knew the like of it anywhere else. And they tell me there isn't the like of it anywhere either. Sure God you should be glad to be getting out of it. There'll be showers of rain racing you all across the channel. Well, are you right now?" He turned to Joe Tunney, who was reaching into his pocket to pay him.

"Well now here you are," Joe said as he handed him the fare, "and that's for yourself."

"Well, I hope I'm here when you come back," the jarvey said to Davy. "God bless you." He climbed back up on the cab and clicked his tongue at the horse. The cab slowly moved away.

The rain came down heavily as we walked quickly toward the shed on the pier. Mrs. McQueen held one of Davy's arms, Audrey the other, and the luggage was held by all. The procession came to the shed and we could see the hull of the mail boat before us. It was the *Cambria*. We could see the name in large letters, yellow-colored on the black hull. Dorry held my hand and then inside the shed she reached over and held her mother's hand, too. The water in the harbor had turned gray. We could hear the sea gulls flying inland, making their calls. There wasn't much talk in the shed, except for soft murmurs. The air was full of cigarette smoke.

The rain came down harder as it began to get even darker. Red tips of cigarettes glowed in the shed. The air became very still. Then the wind came up again and the lightning flashed. A loud thunderclap reverberated up and down the bay. Another flash of lightning and the thunder rolled again. We inched farther back into the shed. Dorry had me stand in front of her. She put her hands on my shoulders and held me against her. The wind blew the rain into the shed. The lightning flashed again. It beat down hard on the seafront road.

There was a movement in the shed. Luggage was picked up and everyone started to move toward the pier. We all stood around Davy and his bride. They stood and looked at us. Around us people were moving toward the entrance and nobody knew what to say. Davy glanced at Audrey, then reached out to Mrs. McQueen, his eyes cast down as if he couldn't look at her. She had set her lips as if to form words that wouldn't come. They put their arms around each other while the crowd still moved past us. There were others saying good-bye, hugging. There were tears and sobs and a child was crying and we still stood around in our circle.

Mrs. McQueen moved back from Davy and then she reached out to Audrey. They hugged and Mrs. McQueen said, "Take care of him." Audrey hugged her and whispered, "I'll write to you." Dorry and all the girls moved closer. They all kissed them and said good-bye. Then Davy turned to me and shook my hand and said, "I must be getting old. I can't pick you up anymore. Or is it that you are growing up so fast?" Audrey put her hand on my head. We all stood back. We watched them in the gloom of the covered pier as they walked toward the gangway. Audrey was carrying the accordion case. Then we saw them disappear into the ship.

"Well, that's that," said Joe Tunney. We turned and started to walk slowly back to the seafront road. Coming out of the covered pier, we could see that it was clearing. There were just some drops falling out over the bay; the sky was

brightening. The strollers came out from under the trees. Steam was rising from the seafront road and the trees were shedding large drops onto the pavements. The sun was starting to brighten everything again with its pale evening light. We could hear the band beginning to play on the promenade. Joe Dolan said, "Isn't that the Belfast reel?"
"Sure I wouldn't know at all," said Mrs. McQueen.

From the road we could see the bay before us. There was a huge rainbow out over the horizon. We heard the blast of the mail boat's whistle and we could see it make its way toward the harbor entrance. It moved slowly in the water and everybody stopped to see it. As it was passing out into the bay, the whistle blew again and it turned to the east and headed out. We could see the crowd standing by the rails and they were waving. We waved back at them and watched the dark ship growing smaller and smaller as it moved eastward through the water. It left a trail of dark smoke behind it and the water was dark, dark blue, nearly purple, the color of Howth. We could just see a touch of white at the bow as it moved farther and farther away. We stood and watched till we could see it no more. The rainbow was gone and the wind started to come up again and Mrs. McQueen said she was cold.

In the autumn we went to Lawlor's Field and looked for walnuts on the way home from school. We climbed over the high iron gates of the home to go to the walnut tree and we threw sticks up at the tree to bring the nuts down. They bounced on the damp earth with a rich thud and we ran and picked them up as if they were made of gold. We stuffed them into our pockets and up our jerseys, rejoicing in our victory.

And once when we were throwing our sticks, the keeper came running up the driveway, shouting. We turned and ran, dropping everything, and climbed over the gate and dropped down to the other side. I fell on my knee and cut it badly. The blood oozed out of a great gash, streaming down my leg. We ran on and on till we thought we were safe and it was only then that I saw my knee. The others crowded around it and stared into the cut. "It's deep, Jackie," they said. "You can see all the way inside."

I was frightened. What was I going to tell my mother? "Sure it's all right," I said. I didn't want to go home. "I can't walk," I told them. They lifted me up, putting my arms over their shoulders.

When we came near the houses a small crowd gathered around us. When they saw my knee they made faces and turned away. I became even more frightened. A rabble of small children followed after us, and I wanted them to go away. Some of them ran ahead of us to announce the news of my knee. My friends carried me to the door of our house. Mary came and opened the door. For an instant she just stared at us. Then she saw my knee and she said, "Oh, my God."

She came down the front steps and put her arms around me, carrying me into the house. "Mammy, Mammy, Jackie has been hurt," she cried. My mother came over to me. She saw the knee and said to my sister, "Put some water on." She sat me in her chair by the fire and came with a towel to wrap around my knee.

"My God how did you do that?"

"I fell."

She took the towel away. It was covered with blood. Then she looked right into my knee. She bit her lip and made a face. "Jesus it's always something," she said, reaching into her apron pocket. She took out some coins and turned to Mary. "Run down to the chemist's and get some lint and bandages."

The blood began to stop. I could feel the heat of the fire on me. The shadow of my outstretched leg flickered on the kitchen wall. It was getting dark, and the lights hadn't been turned on. My mother knelt before me, holding the towel on my knee. I closed my eyes and felt my leg throb.

"You didn't do that from just an ordinary fall," she said. "I'd like to know what you were up to."

"Nothing, I just fell."

She stared at me and I could see her face so clearly. "You'll have me that I'm not worth tuppence," she said. And then she looked at the knee again and she said, "Ah you'll be all right. Ah sure it will be all over like a wedding. All over like a wedding, nothing to it at all."

Every morning before I went to school she dressed my knee. I sat in her chair, and she would take the old bandage off and put a new one on. Sometimes I sat on the kitchen table. The early morning light filled the room, and she always smiled at me. When she bent over my knee I could see down her bosom. I felt that there was some great secret inside it. Sometimes I was afraid to look because of what I might see, as if I could see right through to the center of her and find the place where I had come from. There was a place in there which I knew was secret. It was white, so white and clean, it shined. I knew I wasn't supposed to be looking. There was a place inside her and when I looked down through her bosom I knew I could find it and every time I came close to it I stopped because I was afraid I would never come back. It was as if the secret of life itself were there and I would discover it. It wasn't anything that I could understand, only that it was a secret.

She asked Tommy Roche to walk to school with me every morning because I had to walk slowly. Tommy, who was older, had to walk slowly, too, because one of his legs was shorter than the other. He wore a special boot that was built up to make his legs even, but still his foot turned out and he swayed from side to side when he walked. He had blond hair and his face was full of freckles. He was from a large family that lived near us. He carried a walking stick and he held my hand as we walked. He told me that he hated England. And he told me that when he learned Irish that was all he would speak, "And I don't care whether they understand me or not." His sisters were champion Irish dancers, they had medals and cups, and his big brother, who was much older than him, was called Galway Roche. He wore a gold ring pinned to his coat, which meant that he was a Gaelic speaker. Every morning Tommy came to the house for me and he waited while my mother dressed my knee. "And how is your mother?" she always asked him. "Oh, she's grand, thanks," he'd say.

"And what's this I hear about Galway joining the British army?"

"Ah no, Mrs. Guiney. Sure he hates England."

"Well it must be the German army then."

"It's not the German army either," Tommy told her. "But I know he would go if there was a way of getting there."

I had heard my father say that the Roches were too bloody Irish for his liking. "Sure Jesus with their talking Irish and their dancing and the Gaelic League they give me a pain in the arse," he said. I wished we were more like the Roches.

Every morning on the way to school Tommy told me he had heard the Banshee the night before. "Oh, sure I couldn't sleep at all. She kept waking me up. I was nearly going to throw something at her. She was out there on the green. I looked out the window and I could see her combing her hair. You should see the cut of her. She had a long black dress and her hair was black too, and it came all the way down to her waist and she was looking at the moon and crying and combing her hair. And I'll tell you I know who the Banshee is. And I'll show you, too. Wait till you see." On the way to school we passed some old cottages. They were always known just as the Old Cottages. As we passed them Tommy stopped and then he pointed to the door of one of them and he whispered to me. "She lives in there."

"Is she there in the daytime?" I asked him.

"Sure where else would she be."

"Are you sure that's where she lives?"

"I'm telling you for sure," and just then an old woman came out of the house and Tommy said, "That's her."

"Sure that's only Mag Haley, that's not the Banshee."

"But Mag Haley is the Banshee. That's who I saw crying and combing her hair on the green. I'm telling you for sure it was her."

She walked past us on the road. Her red face was like an Indian's from the weather. She wore slippers on her feet so there was no sound at all when she walked. Her gray hair came out from under the black shawl that covered her head. Her mouth moved as if she were in a conversation with herself. She didn't see the world; she moved silently through it as if she were the only person in it. Her steps were hurried as if she had to be somewhere. Her eyes blazed at the ground with a fierce sorrow, an anguish, and one black stocking hung loosely at her ankle. She had lived in that cottage for as long as I could remember. Every time I saw her I wondered if she had been crying, for at any moment I thought she might sob or wail or tremble with some terrible grief. I often saw her coming up the Hill of Monkstown with an armful of brambles or an old sack over her shoulder. Sometimes when I was passing the cottage she would come to the door with her teapot and empty the leaves onto the road. There was the quietness about her. She passed by on the roads coming and going silently in her grief. I never saw her at mass but often when I would go into the church I saw her kneeling in the front pew looking up at the stained-glass windows over the altar.

"Are you sure she's the Banshee?" I asked Tommy.

"I'm sure she is. My father told me that they let her stay in the cottage so as to keep an eye on her. Didn't you see the big black dog go in and out of the cottage?"

"No. But I saw Smith's donkey in the garden and it was eating her cabbages."

"Well, Smith's donkey and the black dog are the same. You never see the donkey at night and that's because at night the donkey changes into the black dog."

Tommy limped along beside me, and I looked at him. All the dogs of the area had learned through bitter experience to stay away from him. If they came close at all, they got the best of his walking stick or he would lash out at them with his heavy boot.

"Who told you that?" I asked him.

"Jimmy Gillen," he answered.

Jimmy lived in a cottage not far from Mag Haley's. He had a wooden leg because he had been wounded in the troubles. I began to wonder if those who had something wrong with their legs knew more than those who had two good ones. Did they have some special kind of magic? Because I lived near the green and I had never heard the Banshee, nor had I seen the black dog. But Jimmy Gillen had and so had Tommy Roche and they had walking sticks and one had a short leg in a brace and the other had a wooden leg. I wanted to ask Tommy if being able to hear the Banshee had something to do with his leg. But nobody ever mentioned his leg. And nobody ever mentioned Jimmy Gillen's, either. Jimmy had a racing bicycle and it had a special pedal for his wooden leg. When he was about to mount his bicycle everybody had to stand back because he swung the leg around in a great arc and then mounted and fixed his wooden foot in place in the special pedal.

"Sure let me tell you, Jackie," Tommy Roche said to me

one morning. "It's better that you don't know half the things that go on in the middle of the night."

One time something happened in the middle of the day and we all saw it. We were in the schoolyard and it was late in the spring. It was a glorious morning, the sun beaming down. We had been sitting in class when Mrs. Moore, the head teacher, came around and told all the teachers to take everyone out to the yard because it was such a lovely day.

There was a small altar set up on a table at the far wall of the yard. It was there we came for our morning prayers. The table had a white cloth over it and in the center was a statue of the Virgin Mary. She wore a long white robe with a blue sash around the waist. Her head was cast down, the eyes looking at the ground. We brought flowers every day to place at her feet and there were two candles placed on either side of her.

Mrs. Moore always led the prayers and I knew that she really wanted to be a priest. She had prayers at every opportunity and she was always going in and out of Father Sheehan's house. He would often come over to the school to talk to her, and she would look at him with such reverence. She was a terror with catechism, making her own special rounds of the classes to make sure we knew it. She loved to have Father Sheehan examine us because she always knew we would do well. When he said, "Oh, they are marvelous," she smiled with great satisfaction and her thick purple lips rolled back, showing her false teeth.

That morning we all made our way over to the outside altar and stood, and she started the prayers. "The morning offering: O Jesus through the most pure heart of Mary we offer Thee all the prayers, works, and sufferings of this day for all the intentions of Thy Divine Heart." She said the prayers along with us. We could hear her voice above all the others, and she closed her eyes and raised her head. The candles on the altar flickered in the light breeze. I thought there might be a day when we came to the yard and the Virgin's expression might be changed and her head would be lifted up. She seemed to be ashamed or embarrassed, as if she didn't like being looked at. At times I thought I saw a slight movement, perhaps just a twitch of her lip or a blink of her eye. Could she come to life? Would she talk to us as she did to the children at Fatima? Would she give us some terrible secret to bear? Why couldn't there be a miracle right there in the schoolyard? There could be. I didn't have any doubt that the statue could come to life or that my pockets could be suddenly full of coins. God could do anything He wanted. There was nothing that couldn't happen, especially if you asked Him through His mother.

We said the Act of Contrition and then, "Hail Holy Queen. Hail our life our sweetness and our Hope. To thee we cry poor banished children of Eve—Turn them O most gracious advocate thine eyes of mercy toward us." When Mrs. Moore had finished reciting all the prayers, she said, "And now, children, pray silently for your own intentions," and a quietness came over the yard. We could hear carpenters hammering away in the distance, and a dog barked. We prayed on with our heads bowed, our hands joined, but then suddenly there was a cry. "Look, look."

At first I didn't know where to look but then I saw arms pointing to the sky. I saw a long, narrow, white cloud, the only one in the blue sky, and at the tail of the cloud was a great star that shone brighter than any star I had seen at night. It moved slowly across the sky and when it was directly over the altar it seemed to stand still. I heard Mrs. Moore's voice screaming, "Kneel down, children, kneel down." We all knelt down and looked up at the cloud and the star. It had a brightness and a color I had never seen. It was like pure silver, its great points were so long. It twinkled.

The cloud was so white it dazzled us; we had to put our hands over our eyes to shade them. Mrs. Moore started to pray out loud. "Hail Mary full of grace," and we couldn't take our eyes from the sky. The cloud slowly started to move away again. It moved toward the east, and then slowly we all began to stand and look after it. I wanted it to come back; the star kept twinkling so that it seemed to be looking back at us. We watched after it till we could see it no more.

Johnny Seery lived in a cottage near Mag Haley's. Some people said he could do magic and talk to the saints. They said he was older than he looked and that he must be near a hundred. He pumped the organ for the twelve o'clock mass on Sundays. He was small and walked with a limp, his hands clasped behind him. The teeth on one side of his mouth were missing and when he smiled it looked as if he might be mocking. We would always incline our heads as we passed him even if we were in a great hurry, and he always said "Good morra." Sometimes he stood at the door of his cottage, greeting all as they passed. He stood at the door with his waistcoat on and his striped shirt with the collar detached, and we often stood and listened to him tell his stories. Sometimes when we left him, after he had gone back into his cottage, we laughed. There were times when we would see him ahead of us on the road and we would say, "Oh, Jesus, there's Johnny. Let's go the other way." It seemed he always was ahead of us, especially if we were in a hurry.

One Sunday when I had served at the last mass the clerk asked me to wait for a while because there was a woman who had just had a baby who had to be churched. Nearly everyone had left the church when a beautiful young woman came to the altar rail and knelt down. She wore a white lace veil over her head and she was tall, and I could see her long red hair where it hung on her shoulders. Her eyes were bright and she looked as if she was about to smile. Her lovely red cheeks glowed like apples. I knew her name was Jane Evers. She was the sister of Martin Evers, who played football for the Bohemians. All her family sat in the front pew right behind her, and once she glanced back over her shoulder and smiled at them. Everybody knew the Everses. They were rich and handsome, and you never saw just one of them alone. They were always in a great party going somewhere. When they all walked down George's Street they took up all the sidewalk. Her brothers wore the blue and white scarves of Blackrock College. They had the blue blazers, too, but they wore them casually and they didn't show them off.

I stood before her with Father Sheehan, holding the candle while he read the prayers in Latin. Jane Evers bowed her head before the priest, although sometimes she lifted her eyes up and they caught mine and smiled at me. I looked out over her shoulder and I saw her husband, Lorcan Reilly. He wore his officer's uniform, a green jacket and khaki riding breeches with a Sam Browne belt. His face was tanned and his hair was cut short. Everyone knew that his father had been captured during the troubles in 1916 and that he had died in jail.

Father Sheehan said the prayers quietly. Each time I thought he was coming to the end, he turned the page and started again. I thought there was nobody else in the church now except Jane Evers and her family, but when I glanced up I saw Johnny Seery in the balcony, standing at the side of the organ, looking down at the scene below him. His short white hair stood up on his head. His face was pale and he moved his lips. I could only see his face looking down. It seemed to glow in the gloom of the balcony. But Jane Evers's family, who knelt behind her, didn't know that Johnny Seery was looking down on them.

When Father Sheehan came to the end of the prayers, he raised his hand in the blessing and they all bowed their heads. He turned and moved toward the door of the sacristy, and I followed him. Putting my candle down, I came back out to the altar to put the candles out. I looked out past the altar rail where Jane Evers was walking down the aisle with Lorcan Reilly holding her hand and all of her brothers and sisters following behind her. All the red heads of hair and the blue blazers and Johnny was still looking down at them.

As I was leaving the sacristy, Jane Evers and her husband were standing outside talking to Father Sheehan. She laughed and I could hear Lorcan Reilly's voice floating on the soft air. Their laughter echoed against the side of the old church. Father Sheehan was going to dinner with them at their house on the seafront. Jane Evers saw me and smiled. She whispered something to her husband, who then quickly reached into the pocket of his riding breeches, pulled out a handful of coins, and selected two of them. "Stop now a minute. Here you are. That's for yourself."

"Thank you, sir," I said and I looked quickly at Jane Evers. She smiled at me again and as I walked away from them, it was as if I had no legs at all. I could see the tops of the trees down the road out past the church and I could feel my heart beating.

Johnny Seery was on the road ahead of me, walking slowly up the Hill of Monkstown with his hands clasped behind him. It was the quiet hour of the day, Sunday-dinner time when all the families were sitting down to their roasts.

Beyond the crest of the hill were the Dublin mountains dark and blue with light, white clouds hanging over them. I knew I had to pass him. I was hungry and didn't want to slow down to talk to him. I tried to let him get farther ahead of me but I was impatient, and before I was level with him he said without turning, "Them Evers is a fine-looking family." There was nobody else on the road. Sometimes the sun came out from behind the white clouds on the mountains and the light raced toward us down the hill.

We turned off Monkstown Hill, walking toward the cottages. I knew we were nearly home. I would say good-bye to Johnny and then I would start to run. Five minutes from Johnny's cottage, and then I would be home.

But when we came to his cottage he turned to me and said, "Come on in for a minute." I wanted to say no but I couldn't, and he turned up the pathway to the cottage and opened the door.

I walked in after him. It was dark inside. He struck a match and lit the lamp. As the flame slowly rose, I could see the walls. He walked over to the fireplace and started the fire that was laid in the grate, and he stood back looking at it and then he turned to me and smiled.

"As soon as the fire is up I'll make a cup of tea," he said.

"Well, I can't stay long, Johnny," I told him. "I have to be home for dinner."

"Ah, sure I won't keep you long at all. Take your ease now. Sit down." He pointed to a chair at the side of the fire, and he sat down opposite me.

The walls of the cottage were covered with pictures of priests and nuns and bishops and cardinals and there was a framed blessing from the pope. There were saints' pictures, too. St. Francis and St. Anthony and St. Patrick and St. Brigid. There were pictures of people dressed in the clothes worn fifty years ago and not one of them smiled. They looked as if they knew something.

The fire had settled to a soft glow in the grate; shadows danced on the walls. It was like night in the cottage because the windows were covered with heavy curtains and no light came into the house. I began to feel as if the room itself were moving, even as I sat in the chair and could see Johnny looking at me with the same smile on his face.

He picked up the kettle from the hearth, placed it on the fire and then poked it and sat back. I wondered what it was he wanted to talk about. If he would just tell me and let me be on my way. There was a strange smell in the cottage, too. An old, old smell. It was like the smell of the earth itself and the smell of Johnny, too. All the old men had it. I knew that they could see back to times away in the past when things were different. They always stopped to talk to each other. They understood things and they stood back and watched the world. They knew they were in their own time.

Johnny moved the kettle on the fire again. He looked at me and then he bent his head and closed his eyes as if he were trying to remember something. "I knew Lorcan Reilly's father," he said. "Not too many know that. But I knew him. Aye indeed and I did. And there he was in the church this morning with his wife, looking like young toffs. Sure the father wouldn't know them at all. Out of Ringsend he was, a workman like all those around him. No blazers and scarves for him. But a gentleman nevertheless. A true Irishman. Aye he was indeed. Not many knows it but I was with him the night before they caught him. And sure I suppose it doesn't matter anyway."

"Well, what happened, Johnny?" I asked him.

He looked at the fire and the steam was coming out of the kettle. He reached behind him and took down an old silver teapot and put four teaspoons of tea into the pot and poured in the boiling water. He leaned back in his chair. "We'll let that set now." He looked at me and crossed his arms in front of him and gazed down for a moment.

"Well, you know what happened at Boland's Mills. They wouldn't give in and then at last the word came down from Patrick Pearse himself. They were to lay down their arms. Well it was a great disappointment to them because they still had a lot of fight left and to have to surrender to those fellas that couldn't beat them squarely was a hard thing. But they were all ordered to leave and come out and there they were surrounded by Tommies and they were all marched off. Except for Lorcan Reilly. He hid himself and was covered with some old flour sacks and they never found him and he waited until it was dark and then he made his way out. But it was hard to move. Dublin was crawling with Tommies but he got into the snug of a pub he knew and they gave him an old overcoat and out he was again and what did he do but wait for a tram. That's what he did. And you don't know this now but it was your grandfather was driving the tram and didn't he put Lorcan up on the top of it and he wouldn't allow anyone else up there and he told them there was a priest up there with a dying man. Your grandfather knew Lorcan because he was from Ringsend, too. They went to school together. Well, they let Lorcan off at the York Road in Kingstown and Paddy Redmond the conductor takes him up to Tom Kelly's forge. Down the lane beside the slaughterhouse and Tom was still there and he hid him in the back of the forge. Ah but they got him. They did. The next day didn't they come right to the forge as if they knew he was there. They took him away and he never was to see his wife nor his son again. And that's what I was thinking when I looked down from the balcony today. To see young Lorcan sitting there surrounded by the scarves and the blazers. Aye, he died in the prison in England and he never saw the wife nor the child again. I brought him some grub that night in the forge. Tom Kelly came here and got me. Sure you would never know who saw what."

He poured some tea into his cup and stirred it with his spoon that was stained brown. Then he picked it up and blew into it and took a small sip.

"Not many knows that story," he said. "Not many knows. There was your grandfather and Paddy Redmond and Tom Kelly and meself. And I don't know why but we never said a word of it to anyone. Never a word of it. And I would see them and we would have a jar and an auld chat from time to time but none of us ever mentioned Lorcan Reilly. It was only seeing the son today and knowing who he was brought it all back to me. But he looks more like the mother and I never knew her at all or where she was from or who her people were. There was none of the wrap-the-green-flag-round-me with the likes of your grandfather. Decent men. They knocked out their own living."

Johnny drank his tea and he gazed into the fire. "Sure there's things I could tell you but people would think I'd be romancing or that I'd have gone mad. They believe what they see and no more. Oh, but I could tell them. If I ever started to tell them what I have seen around here and up in the mountains. They think I'm daft as it is. Oh, I know what they do be saying. Passing me by on the roads. Here's Johnny, they say. Sure I never cared one way or the other whether they passed me by or not."

I could see the reflection of the fire in his eyes. I looked into it, too, to see what I could see but there was only the white ashes of the turf, the red glow and the gray smoke curling up the chimney.

"I better go, Johnny," I said to him and he slowly turned his head. I stood up and moved toward the door. "Take a look at that picture of St. Patrick," he said. "It's got his hymn on the back of it." I looked at the picture and there stood the patron. "I was given this picture a long long time ago. God, it must be fifty years ago now. Old Canon Doherty gave it to me. God be good to him. Aye he was up there in Cabinteely for years and my mother was his housekeeper. When the canon died he left my mother a little sum and didn't he leave the picture to me. And when I took it down off the wall I saw the hymn on the back of it. Written in all the old Irish letters."

He took the picture down off the wall and he turned it over. I could see the lovely old Celtic design and the words stood out in all their colors. *"Hail glorious Saint Patrick, dear saint of our Isle. On us thy poor children, bestow a sweet smile."*

I couldn't take my eyes off the words.

"And did you ever hear tell of the promise of St. Patrick?" he asked.

"No," I said, looking at him.

"Well the way they tell it is that when the end of the world is coming, St. Patrick has asked God to let Ireland slip under the sea and be drowned and not be destroyed by fire like the rest of the world. I suppose it's better to go that way than to be burned. They say drowning is the best way to go. You hear lovely music and you just sort of slip away with no bother at all. Ah, well, we're not done yet. But when it's time for me to go I might just go down to the harbor and let meself into the water. Peaceful. No bother."

I opened the door and I turned and said good-bye and he took a few steps after me and then he stood in the doorway. He looked up and down the road, holding his hands out in front of him with the palms turned up to see if it was raining.

Dinner was nearly over when I got home.

"What kept you?" my mother asked me.

"There was benediction and there was a woman being churched and then I had to walk home with Johnny Seery."

"Now you didn't have to walk home with Johnny Seery. You needn't have if you didn't want to. Walking home with old Johnny would put years on you."

I wanted to tell them all the things Johnny had said to me about Grandad and the tram and Lorcan Reilly.

"And what did Johnny have to say?" my father asked me. "Did he tell you about all the things he saw up in the mountains? Ah sure poor Johnny is harmless. God, he'd keep you for hours."

"Who was being churched?" my mother asked.

"Lorcan Reilly's wife," I told her. "And he gave me five shillings."

"Well now," my father said, "he wouldn't be Lorcan Reilly's son if he didn't. There was no one like the father. There was a man could have been the leader of this country, not like the other fool we have in there now. Give a workingman a chance and they'd see the way things should be run."

I heard what my father had said—"Johnny is harmless"—and I wanted to believe all that Johnny had told me and nothing would ever change it.

Long after my knee had healed, Tommy Roche still walked to school with me. One morning he told us his leg was paining him and they were going to have to get him a new boot and a brace. My mother said she didn't like the look of him. She thought he was getting thinner and she said he looked pale. He hadn't changed for me. He still became very quiet when he saw Mag Haley. He still told me of the nights when he heard her crying on the green.

One morning his sister came over and said he wouldn't be going to school for a few days because he was sick. I missed walking to school with him and when I saw Mag Haley I thought of him and wondered if she was really the Banshee. Then one morning in the schoolyard just before the morning prayers Mrs. Moore told us all to say a special prayer for Tommy Roche because he was very sick. We said three Our Fathers and three Hail Marys. Some of the older children said that he was dying. They had a funeral when you died and people never saw you again and you were buried. It was just something that happened, and I knew it was the opposite of alive.

Before we left the school that day we learned that Tommy had died. I passed his house on the way home. There was a small white card with a black border pinned to the front door. It said: Thomas Michael Roche. Died Twentieth November, 1947. Aged Eleven Years. R.I.P.

When I got home I told my mother and she said she knew and it was very sad. "I thought for a long time he was failing," she said. "I could see it in his face. He was a good boy. God help his poor mother. He's in heaven with the angels. Far better off he is, too."

Some of us went to the house to see Tommy after he was laid out. He was in bed by himself, looking as if he were asleep. His hands were joined over his breast and they held a white rosary, and his face was clear and small. His brothers and sisters sat downstairs in the living room talking in whispers. Sometimes I could hear a quiet cry or a sob. We all knelt and said a decade of the rosary together and I thought of Tommy lying in the bed. His mother had come to the side of the bed when we were there and she knelt down and looked at him and whispered. She was a big woman and her large bosom stood out from her and hung over Tommy. She sighed and looked down at him and then she held onto the edge of the bed and pulled her head into her breast and closed her eyes.

The next day the hearse came, pulled by two black horses. The coffin was carried down the path and then placed in the back of the hearse. It was taken to the church where it was kept for the night, and at devotions that evening I saw it standing all by itself in the vestibule with four lighted candles around it. I wondered what he looked like inside the coffin. Was he still the same?

The next day when I was at school I heard the bell tolling and then the sound of the horses as the procession passed by on the way to the cemetery.

Whenever I saw Mag Haley I wondered if she knew that Tommy was dead. At night when I lay in my bed I listened to hear if she was crying on the green. I thought that if I heard her I would die, too. But there was only the quietness of the night with the wind in the great beech trees at the back of the house. And then I could hear my father's snores and I was glad. Sometimes he would talk out loud in his sleep. He said other men's names and he shouted and then suddenly it would all stop and be quiet again. And then I could hear the wind.

It snowed the year Tommy died. There was hardly any coal or wood to be had for fires. When I came home from school my hands were so cold my mother would wash them in hot water. The pain came when they started to warm again and the blood began to flow through them. In the mornings when I came down the stairs and went into the kitchen I saw her kneeling beside the fireplace cleaning the grate, picking out the pieces she could burn again. When the coal boats arrived from England, they docked at the trawlers' piers at the foot of the York Road. Soon a great procession of hand-carts started out for the coal yards in the hope that there would be enough to go around. My mother would always say to us, "There's a boat in. See if you can get down to the yard before it's all gone." We wore old stockings on our hands for gloves and we took the handcart from the back of the house and started on our journey.

We tried shortcuts to get to the yards as fast as we could. Down the Hill of Monkstown and up the Willy Gambols Hill and down the York Road and always when we got to the yard the line stretched out to the street with every variety of handcart. We stood at the end of the line, stamping our feet on the cobblestones, trying to keep warm, looking ahead at the mountain of coal and hoping it wouldn't be all gone before it was our turn. We saw the great dray horses standing in the shafts of their wagons as they were loaded up and we knew that the rich houses had it delivered. The draymen's faces were blackened from the coal dust. They wore their caps on the sides of their heads and it looked as if the caps were permanently flattened into place from carrying the dark sacks of coal. They were like hunchbacks, and their red lips held the small butts of cigarettes.

We saw Beardy Russell, who owned his own dray. He had a red beard and a great red mustache curled up at the ends. His face was never as blackened as the others. He was tall and handsome. They said that all the women were mad for him and he was mad for them, too. When the carnival had been held up in Sutton's Field there was a huge tent for dancing and once when I crept in under it I saw Beardy Russell putting his hand up a girl's dress and she was telling him not to do that but he wouldn't stop. He kept telling her she didn't mind at all and she laughed at him and tried to hold onto his arm. "We'll be seen," she told him. "Let them look," he said. "Let them have a bloody good look."

When I passed him on the roads sitting on the top of the

coal sacks on his wagon with the reins in his hands, he winked at me and I wondered if he knew me. I knew he liked Dorry McQueen. He was always after her to go out with him but she never did. On Sundays when he wore his pin-striped suit and his bow tie, you'd never know he was a coal man at all. He looked like a picture star.

As we got closer to the coal, the mountain was nearly gone. They filled our sack with slack and they had some turf left, too, and we were glad that we had something to bring home.

As we left the coal yard, it began to get dark and colder. The snow was hard and icy, and Paul stood between the shafts of the handcart. We began the journey home. The load became heavier as we made our way up the York Road, and when the hill became steeper our feet slipped from under us on the icy snow. We fell and the cart stood still. Paul cursed. He told me to take the shafts and he pushed and we started to move up the hill but he slipped again and hit his chin on the cart. Blood oozed from his mouth because he had bitten his tongue. He stood and cursed and held his tongue between his lips. The curses sounded funny, the way he had to say them with his tongue cut. I looked at him and laughed. He sat down on the side of the road and I still laughed. He leaped up from where he was sitting and chased me up the hill while the cart stood in the road. I ran up the hill ahead of him. He stopped and sat down again with his head between his knees and I came back down and stood before him. He didn't look up. I could see my breath on the air and the stars were coming out now in the twilight. The sky was fiery red and dark blue. The trees stood still at the side of the road. He looked up wearily and I could see the blood on his lips. He stared out in front of him for a while and then he slowly stood and moved to the handcart. He looked back over his shoulder and said "Push," and we started up the hill again. Slowly the wheels turned and we made our way up the hill. The evening stood still around us. We could feel the cold settling in for the night. The blue and the red of the twilight danced around our heads as we moved together to the rhythm of the cart.

As we approached the top of the hill we saw a line of Christian Brothers black against the snow, all wearing their hats and their gloves. Their faces were red. When they saw us, Brother Mallon came over. He saw Paul's lip and asked him what had happened and then he told him to be careful. Paul was in his class and they always said he was fair. We passed the house where the brothers lived and we could see the lights in the windows and the smoke from the chimneys. Across the road was the Convent of Mercy. It stood locked and quiet and far away from the world. We passed the horse trough in Monkstown before we made our way down the Willy Gambols Hill, and it was frozen. The old iron trough was painted green and we came panting up to it like horses ourselves. It was dark. We started down the hill and we had to hold the cart back because it wanted to fly down by itself. It fought to get away from us and we were running to keep up with it. I had to let go and then it pushed Paul down the hill and I ran after them. He ran like a sprinter and the cart behind threatened to run over him. Then toward the end of the hill one of the wheels came flying off and went on a mad journey of its own. The cart skidded, the bare axle dug into the snow and it came to a sliding halt and turned over on its side. Paul had let go of the shafts and his momentum carried him way past the cart like a runner finishing a race.

We were at the bottom of the hill and over on the side was Wheeler's Swamp and Monkstown Castle standing darkly in the gloom. We could barely see the trees, which stood up from the swampy ground. We started to look for the wheel.

When it rolled in the snow we hadn't heard any sound at all. We walked up and down the ditches at the side of the road and Paul cursed. He kicked the snow and picked up the dead branches and flung them aside. I copied him and flung the branches aside, too, but underneath it all I had a great urge to laugh. "Jesus, we'll never get home," he said. I moved toward the gates of the castle and, hiding behind the great stone pillar of the gate, I put my forehead against the coldness and started to shake with laughter. I laughed as if I had a companion. The tears ran down my cheeks and I shook against the wall. I thought I would choke. Every time I thought of Paul running down the hill I convulsed again. I put my hands out in front of me and held onto the pillar for support. I heard Paul shouting, "I found it. I found it," but still the laughter was in my throat. I brushed the tears away from my eyes and the convulsions still rumbled inside of me.

Paul was standing over the cart with the wheel in his hand. He looked at me and he thought I had been crying.

"It's all right now," he said. "We'll be home soon." We went up the hill of Monkstown and we put the coal in the shed at the back of the house. My mother was glad. She stood at the back door with the steam rising from her arms because she had been doing the wash. She smiled and she said, "You got it. Aren't you great!"

Many things I didn't understand happened that year. I wondered at times why there was anger or tears or doors slammed shut or why there were whispers. It was the year one of my grandfathers died. He was the one I never saw because he lived in Wicklow and he never came to Dublin. A telegram came to the house to say that he had died, and the next day my father took the bus to Gortmore. The day he came back, we were all put out of the kitchen. We sat in the living room and listened, wondering what was wrong. I could hear my mother say, "It's all right, Johnny, it's all right. Let them have it. Let them have it." And then I heard my father say, "But it was all done before I got there. Be Jesus they didn't even wait till he was in the grave. All done before I got there. I'd have given it to them." Then I heard his fist come down on the table with a terrible crash and I heard the dishes break and my mother pleading with him.

"Would you believe them," he said. "Joe Gormley told me they put the pen in my father's hand. Sure Jesus how could he know what he was doing. Wouldn't you think he would even ask me? But he never asked me anything anyway. People leading him around all his life. Just the same way he let Nellie Potter send us away when we were children. Jesus he was true to form to the end."

We sat in the living room listening in silence. Every time I went to ask Paul what was going on, he glared at me and told me to be quiet. He made his way to the kitchen door and put his ear against it and I wanted to go there, too, but he shook his fist at me and I went back and sat on the couch. I could hear the voices go on, low and intimate just between the two of them. My mother's voice was gentle and soft. The kitchen door opened and Paul came scurrying back to the living room. My father came out with the newspaper in his hand and sat down on the sofa as if we were not there. He held the paper out in front of him and didn't look at us. Then my mother appeared at the door and said, "Come on now outside. Give your father some peace. The sun is out. Go up to Boley and see if you can find me some brambles for the fire."

I walked with Paul to the Boley Woods, and he was angry. I had to trot to keep up with him. He looked straight ahead, his eyes fixed and his head bent forward in anger. He started muttering to himself and I strained to hear what he said. "What are you saying, Paul?" I asked him. He didn't answer, and when I asked him again, he glowered at me.

I wondered what he had heard. What could have made him so angry? He was always angry when my father came into the house and sometimes he muttered things under his breath. His eyes fell to the floor when my father looked at him. There were times when Paul had said things to my mother about my father, and one day she told him not to talk about him like that. "It doesn't make any difference what he does. When you earn enough to put the food on the table and pay the rent then you can open your mouth but not until then. And let me tell you, me bucko, there is few like your father. Aye indeed, few like him and isn't he entitled to his few pints? He doesn't deprive us. Bloody back-breaking job he does, up at four every morning. Oh, no, me bucko. I won't hear that from you nor anyone else either. You won't talk about your father like that, not in this house nor anywhere else either."

Paul had his hands in the pockets of one of our uncle's old railway uniform jackets that had been cut down but was still too large. It flapped around him as the wind came racing across the field. I could see the trees in the Boley Woods, black and bare, rising above the snow at the edge of the field. We climbed over the low wall and entered the woods. Paul opened the sack he was carrying and we started to search for the brambles.

The winter stillness stared at us as we moved quietly up the small path through the trees. I still wanted to ask him why he was so angry. He stopped to pick up some brambles and gave me the sack to hold. I carried it over my shoulder as we moved up the path.

"I want to show you something but you are not to tell anyone," Paul said. He led me through the woods until we came to a small clearing, and then we took a path I had never seen before. We came to a low hut made of sods that was off the path built against the stable walls of Sir Valentine Grace's house. There was a small opening, hardly big enough for a body to squeeze through. Paul went in on his hands and knees and I followed him. He found matches and lit a candle. I saw his face leaning over it as he placed it in a holder so I could see. There were old milk crates for seats and on the walls were pictures of football teams. Old doormats served as carpets. The hut smelled of earth and tea and tobacco. There were old cigarette butts on the floor and on the wall there was a drawing of a black swastika. The stable wall was of stone, and even in the darkness of the hut I could see the sweat rolling down the stone to the floor. There was a small window made out of the glass cover of a biscuit tin, and it looked out at the trees.

Paul sat down with his back to the wall and looked at me. I felt good that he had brought me to this secret place. He lifted one of the milk crates, and underneath it was a pack of cigarettes. He took one out, lit it from the candle and then took a deep drag. Tilting his head back, he blew the smoke toward the roof of the hut. "You are too young to smoke yet," he said. "This is where me and Davin and Roe come to meet and talk. Nobody knows about this place, only us. Never tell anyone you were here. I wouldn't have brought you except I needed a cigarette." I was glad he wasn't angry. "What do you think of it?" he asked me. I nodded and smiled.

Davin and Roe were his friends, and I had often heard the three of them talking at night as they stood outside our house under the bedroom window. They argued, scoffing and jeering at each other, but mostly they talked about going to the secondary school. They all wanted to go. Mallon had told them to urge their parents to send them. You had to pay to go there and rarely did anyone from the national schools go, but Mallon kept urging them. Paul wanted to go. Sometimes Billy McAuley joined them and they listened to him because he was already in the secondary. He told them the names of the brothers, who was good and who was hard. He told them about Virgil and about the homework and the operetta they were going to put on. They always said that Paul was the smartest. "Guiney has you all beat," I heard Davin say one day. "Even Mallon himself says it." And I heard my mother tell my father that Mallon had sent her a note about Paul. He told her that Paul was the brightest boy in the class and he told her to do everything she could to send him to the secondary. My father didn't say anything. My mother went to the kitchen and said softly, "Oh, it's easy for them. Easy for them to tell us what to do. Why couldn't they give him a scholarship. They would never think of anything like that." She had said it for my father because she knew how he felt.

Paul puffed his cigarette and leaned his head back against the wall. I could see his teeth, the crooked one in the front. I wanted him to look at me and laugh the way he used to. He used to smile at me and I wanted him to make me feel the way he did when he came into our bedroom at night. I was never happy until he was there. I wondered what was wrong. He looked at me and then turned away again. "What, Paul?" I asked him. He looked at the butt between his fingers and he took a final pull. He threw it against the far wall. My eyes followed it across the hut. It hit the wall and fell to the ground and lay there with the blue smoke still rising from it, its red end facing us.

"I'm never going to the secondary," Paul said. "I wonder why I ever hoped to." He picked up a small twig from the floor and flung it at the wall.

"Why can't you go, Paul?"

"Oh, I don't know." He kicked out with his foot. "Because we can't afford it."

He looked at me and swallowed. He clenched his teeth and started to breathe heavily, then jumped to his feet and kicked out at a milk crate, sending it flying. "Because our father wouldn't go after what's his own. They took the fields from him down there in Wicklow and he let them have it. He let them take them. And him coming home drunk every night. He doesn't know Ma has to work to keep us going. And she telling us he doesn't deprive us. And it's not that he doesn't make the money. He makes more than all the men around here. Who else works like him? Look by the fireplace every night and you'll see the betting tickets torn up for all the horses that never came in. Did you ever hear anything like him? Every day the same story." He began to mimic him. "'O Jesus I was going to put the money on the winner but Jim Fogarty told me he had a tip and I changed my mind at the last minute. Why the hell did I listen to him.' Jesus, how many times have we heard that one?

"And look. Look." He bent down to show me the torn toecap of his boot hanging loose, and I could see his foot in the boot. "Not enough money in the house for a pair of boots but your man home drunk every night. Jesus, he's the one who isn't deprived. I was playing in a match with Davin and Roe and all of them and I was the only one who didn't have a pair of football boots. I saw our father standing down by the goalposts watching. He must have seen me running around the field with the toecap hanging off my boot like a bloody horse with a loose shoe. Sure Jesus I could still run rings around all of them even with the toe hanging off my boot. And did you ever hear him about the scarves and the blazers?" He began to mimic our father again. "'Bloody crowd of them that goes to the secondary be Jesus with the scarves and the blazers and the arses out of their trousers and them starving for the want of a good meal. By Christ none of you leave this house hungry. You can never say that. None of you ever left this house hungry and don't you forget it.'"

I stared at him and I didn't know what to say, and then he said softly, "I'd rather be hungry once in a while and be able to go to school. It's not the money with him. He'd find it if he wanted to. It's the scarves and the blazers." His eyes stared blankly ahead of him, and he looked drunk himself. For an instant I wanted to laugh. The look of pain and outrage on his face was comical. It was as though my father were playing a joke on him. His hair hung down over his eyes, and he bit his bottom lip in the same way my mother did. I felt a gust of wind against the hut; the candle flickered quickly. I saw the shadow of his head and shoulders on the wall. I looked through the tiny window and saw that it was starting to snow again. Big flakes were falling slowly. "We better go," he said, and we walked down through the field together.

After that, Davin and Roe and Paul still talked under the window at night. They still laughed and jeered at each other but they didn't talk about the secondary anymore, and even in the house, Paul never mentioned it. They were always knocking at the front door for him, looking for him to go out, and they laughed their way down the avenue. He didn't talk to me anymore when he came home. When I whispered, "Hello, Paul," he'd say, "Aren't you asleep yet? Go to sleep," and he never told me where he had been.

And then they all had to go to court. Davin and Roe and Paul and McAuley and a crowd of others, too. They all went off that morning with their mothers. When I looked out the window it was like a parade the way they all walked silently together. They wore their Sunday suits and there was not a word said about why they all had to go. One day when I had walked into the kitchen, Paul and my mother had stopped talking. Once Mary and my mother had whispered, too, and became quiet when they saw me. At other times there were strained whispers. Every once in a while a word would break through and then, as if there had been a violation, there would be another long silence, and after a while, the whispers again.

It had begun to rain early that morning and the skies were that awful dull gray that seemed to hang over us in those winter months and stare down with all the loneliness that was ever in the world. There was no wind and the rain came straight down, relentless and angry and indifferent, running in torrents through the gutters. Everything was damp and the sweat ran down the walls. My tweed jacket smelled of rain and the glass cover on the face of the clock in the classroom was clouded so we couldn't tell the time. The bell in the tower in the town hall struck the half-hour, ringing out so clearly that morning. I could hear the trams moving on George's Street and the horses' hooves on the cobblestones, the sound of tires on the wet streets as the cars passed by.

Mr. Martin had us read and we were quiet. All the other classes were quiet, too. The pigeons sat on the window ledge looking in at us, rustling their wings self-consciously. When Mr. Martin spoke it was in a low voice, as if he didn't want to disturb the quietness which covered the town.

I thought of Paul and my mother and I wondered why they were in the court. I had seen my father talking to Mr. Fay, the policeman up the avenue. They had stood at the top of the road near the dairy, and Mr. Fay spoke low and intently to him. My father followed his face as he spoke and bent forward, shaking his head. Mr. Fay kept saying, "Now, Johnny, now, Johnny, listen to me. For God's sake listen to me."

The rain stopped in the afternoon and it was colder. Everyone said the roads would freeze so we made plans on the way home to make a slide that night. I had forgotten about the court and when I walked up the path to the house Mary opened the door before I knocked, as if she had been watching for me. The kitchen door was closed and she brought me into the living room. "Stay in here," she said, and then she sat and looked at me.

I heard my father's voice. It rose up and grew louder as he spoke and then he was shouting. "All guilty, all guilty. All for that bitch. It's not right. Fay knows it. They all know it. Bloody ferret-faced bitch. Every lad that lives on the road guilty because of her. All you have to do is look at that bitch of a woman."

"O Johnny, Johnny, it's over and done with," my mother said. "And what harm came of it? They were all let go."

"Aye, all let go," my father said, "after being dragged into court and made to stand there on account of that bitch. What the hell goes on in Boley? She must have been in there with them. She says she was. Molesting her, was it? Is that what she said? Is it? That's some bloody crowd for you to be caught with. All the bright fellows."

I heard the chair scrape the floor and fall over. My mother was pleading with him. I heard the brass fender from the fireplace bang against the wall, then the sound of quick steps and my father said, "Look at him. Look at him. The philosopher from under the window. Be Jesus how could you be tied up with anything has to do with that bitch? You that's so bloody smart. Aye, and Davin and Roe, too. And they the ones going to the secondary. See where it gets them."

"It will get them where I'll never be," Paul shouted.

I couldn't believe that he dared speak to my father like that. The kitchen door rattled as if someone were trying to break through it, and then I heard my mother's voice and she was pleading. "O Johnny, Johnny, for God's sake sit down. Johnny, Johnny, don't go near him. Johnny please."

"Bloody little cur," my father shouted. "You prig. Bloody prig. You and the bloody secondary. If I get my hands on you you'll never spend another day in any school. Come out from behind your mother. Come out. Be Jesus I'll scuttle ye."

"Jesus Mary and Joseph," my mother screamed. The kitchen door opened and she shouted, "Get out, get out," and Paul came rushing out into the hallway and ran out the front door and down the path. The gate slammed after him and he was gone. The kitchen door slammed shut again, and then the house was silent.

Mary and I looked out the living-room window. The streetlight on the corner had come on and the wind was blowing through the hedges around the front of the house. We looked for Paul through the darkness but he was gone. Then we looked at each other and we began to cry. I moved my chair closer to Mary and we sat together in the silence, looking into the fire. She held my hand and put her arm around my shoulder and she shook as she cried. She was dark like my father. She had his eyes, too, but she was so gentle. She never shouted or got angry.

We heard the kitchen door open and then my father going up the stairs slowly. They creaked under him. I heard the bedroom door open and he was gone. I looked at Mary. She stood up and tiptoed to the kitchen, and I followed her. My mother looked up when she saw us. She smiled quickly and turned away. Her face was red. Pushing the gray hair back from her forehead, she put her finger to her lips to tell us to be quiet. We sat with her. She stared into the fire and after a while we heard my father's snoring. "Is Paul outside?" she asked us.

"We couldn't see him," Mary said.

"Where could he have gone and he without a coat and he didn't have his dinner either." She walked to the front door and looked out. The light from the house streamed into the garden. "God it's cold." She folded her arms around her as she stared out into the night. There was a huge moon in the sky with a great circle around it. The white clouds sped past it, turning it on and off, and I could hear the shouts and the laughter of the crowd making the slide on the road. I wondered if Paul was with them.

"I'll go and see if he is down by the slide," I said.

I looked for Paul's white shirtsleeves and red pullover. Figures came running past me on the way to the slide. I walked the length of the ice but he wasn't there. The air was full of shouts, and in the sharp cold I could see the breath of the sliders hanging in the air where they stood in clusters with the scarves tied over their heads to keep their ears warm. I walked back to the house. My mother was still at the door, and when she saw me she shook her head. I shook mine in reply. She turned and went inside and I followed her and we sat by the fire.

We could hear the steady rhythm of my father's snores. They came from deep inside him, each one like the one before. My mother knitted and stared. Mary brought her a cup of tea. She looked at us, holding the cup in her two hands. Her green eyes were soft and gentle. She looked lost, moving her lips as if she wanted to say something. She took a sip from the cup and closed her eyes. "He'll die his death of cold," she said. "Where could he have gotten to?"

I thought about the hut in the Boley Woods. Could he be there? "I know where he is," I said, and I jumped up from my place at the fire. "Where?" they both said at once. "I bet he is up in the Boley Woods," I said. "Well, go up there and bring him his coat and tell him to come home," my mother said. "Be careful," Mary shouted after me.

I went out into the night, carrying his coat. When I looked

past the streetlight I saw the figures hurtling down the slide, and scarves flying in the air behind them. I turned away from them, and as I walked toward the field, their cries grew faint behind me.

The moon disappeared behind the clouds as I started to walk across the field. The hard snow crunched under my feet. I looked through the darkness for the place where I could go over the wall. The wind in the trees rose and fell with a terrible moan.

I felt my way over the wall and stood peering into the woods. I looked for the light from the hut but there was only the darkness. Branches scraped against me and reached out as if to draw me in to them. My heart was beating against my chest, the sound of it echoing in my ears. I tried to link my thoughts to Paul's to let him know that I was there. Then I thought I heard my father's voice over the sound of the wind in the trees. "Leave him be. Leave him be." I stopped and I listened, but it was only the wind.

I followed the narrow path, darkness all around me. I wanted to call out for Paul but it was as though I had no voice. I knew he would be angry when I found him; I knew he would tell me to go home. I heard Sir Valentine Grace's setters barking in the distance and I wondered if they could hear me. Then I saw a dim light off the path, through the trees, and I started to walk toward it. It seemed to flicker on and off as the wind moved the branches. It was amber and delicate, twinkling like a small star, so fragile that I thought if I looked too hard it would disappear.

When I came up to the window and looked in, I saw him. He was smoking and staring at the candle. I wanted to tap on the window to let him know that I was there but I could only stare in at him. I felt his jacket in my hands and knew he would be glad of it. He turned his head and stared at the window. At first he didn't see me but suddenly he leaped up and his face was staring at me. He had that look I was afraid of. I held his jacket up to the window and then he motioned angrily to me to come into the hut. When I got to the entrance he pulled me in roughly and I went flying across the hut and landed on the floor. "I brought your jacket," I said. His eyes stared past me as if they didn't see me. Then in an instant he reached down and snatched the jacket from me and put it on.

"Mammy says you're to come home," I said to him in a whisper. I sat on the floor where I was and looked up at him.

He rubbed his arms, then he blew into his hands and he shivered. "I'm not going home. I'm going to stay here or I'll just go off on the roads. They won't know where I am. I'll be gone. I'll be in the mountains."

"Oh, come home, Paul," I said, and I started to cry to myself and I turned my head away from him because I didn't want him to see. I felt the sob rise in my throat and I tried to hold it down but it exploded and burst out of me.

He turned to look at me with his fury and the tears fell from me onto the floor of the hut. "Shut up, will ye," he said. "Shut up. Shut up," and he put his hands on my shoulders and shook me. "Stop it. Stop it." He stared into my face and then the sobs began to ease and I reached up with my jacket sleeve to wipe my eyes.

He stared at the wall. "Jasus," he kept saying, "Jasus," in the same way my father said it.

"Are you going to come home?" I asked him again. He looked at me and shivered. "Daddy is in bed," I told him. "Mammy wants you to come home. Oh, come on, Paul. He's asleep. He won't even know you are in the house. He won't even hear you. Come home. Come home."

He still stared at the wall, his hands on his hips. He leaned to one side and turned his head in anguish. We could hear the wind blowing against the hut and we both shivered in the cold dampness. The setters were still barking; we could hear them above the sound of the wind. The candle flickered, casting our shadows in different directions. He turned and looked at me and then he bowed his head. I thought he was going to cry. He reached down with his hand and I reached out to him and he helped me up. We went out into the woods together and I walked behind him down the path, afraid that I would lose him in the dark. The trees swayed around us, watching us make our way through them. I had such a feeling for him, wanting him to be happy, and I hoped he would never go away again.

When Paul and my father were in the house together after that they never said much to each other. My mother was always ready to jump between them. She steered them away from each other, and there were times when everyone forgot and we could laugh together. Sometimes my father would read an article from the newspaper out loud to us and then we would talk about it. When it was funny he would start to laugh before he got to the end of it. Sometimes Paul would raise his eyes in disdain. Then my mother would catch his eye and look at him with a warning on her face. It was a pleading to him to keep the peace. Paul would make a remark or he would disagree. And with Paul it wasn't that he disagreed so much as it was his way. He had a tone of voice he used, and he raised his head and looked up to the ceiling as if he was sure we wouldn't understand what he was saying. He lectured to us with a little grin that would come upon him when he had made his point. I could see my father clench his fists or hold his hands tightly together and he would sometimes glare at Paul. Then he usually left the kitchen and went up to bed without saying good night. Paul would grin at us after he had left and my mother would be angry at him. "Mr. Smart Fellow," she would say. "Always ready to bring the end to a good thing. Jesus, you love to make trouble. It isn't often that your father is mellow enough to sit down with us and have a laugh. Be Jesus you'd rile the divil himself. Sometimes you can be a bloody cur." And all the while Paul smirked.

There were many long silences, too, when neither of them dared say a word. My mother would look from one to the other, with pleading in her face, but if either one of them had to make a point then nothing would stop them. Nobody was happy on those nights.

There was a night when my father had told a story about the Black and Tans up in Cabinteely. He told us about how they had come through the village and gotten them all out of bed at two in the morning and then put the bucket on old Charlie Rooney's head and sent him running down the street. He couldn't see where he was going and they were shooting their rifles over his head.

And then he told us about the true British soldier. The Tommy. "Oh, there's nothing like your true Tommy. No harm in them at all. Likes his pint like the rest of us and his laugh and an auld singsong. Oh, they were a decent crowd for the most. No, it was the bloody Black and Tans did the worst. A terrible lot. Bloody dirt. Your Tommy was a different sort altogether. Loved a good laugh. Jesus I'll never forget the time I was walking up the Marine Road of a summer night. It was still light out and the usual summer crowd was walking home from the pier. The Marine Road was crowded. Well, Jesus, I hear a cheer and I look up the road and what do I see but two Tommies. One is pulling a handcart down the road and other is sitting on the back of it, and be Jesus the fellow pulling is running like a hare down the road. Well he goes all the way down to the end of the road and without stopping the two of them and the cart go right into the harbor. Well you never saw anything like it in your life. It was like Charlie Chaplin. To this day every time I think of it I start to laugh."

We were all laughing with him and he had his head thrown back and the laughter was coming out of him. His mouth was wide open and he was wiping the tears away from his eyes. They came so easily when he laughed. Paul had been outside of the talk, not paying any attention, with his head in a book and his chair pulled over to the side, but he was laughing, too. He had tried his best not to laugh and he had even clenched his fist and put it up to his mouth but then he couldn't hold it back and he was laughing like the rest of us. My mother laughed and her face got redder and her knitting dropped from her lap and fell on the hearth. We all felt good. Then my father said good night and went up to bed. I heard him winding the alarm to be up at four for work in the morning. He called down the stairs to remind my mother to leave his clean work clothes out. "Leave the singlets and the trousers out, Kelly," he said, and then in a short time we could hear him snoring. On and on he went and I was so glad because I knew he was home and safe and in bed.

The fire was red and soft and peaceful with the white ashes creeping out to the fender, the low flames gently sputtering. The hall clock ticked on, its strong beat never changing, on and on every second like my father's snores, reaching every room in the house. I could feel the house itself settling down, comfortable, happy, and peaceful, feeling itself and us in it as if it would always take us safely to some place. My mother's knitting needles scraped against each other, and we listened to the snores ringing through the house. He was a stranger known to us all lying in his bed and he was all around us.

Suddenly there was a loud crash from upstairs. We were stunned, and then we heard my father cry out in great pain, "Cathleen, Cathleen." We all went running up the stairs. My mother got there first and I heard her say, "Jesus Mary and Joseph, Johnny, what happened?" My father couldn't talk, he could only moan, and when I came into the room I saw him lying on the floor with the night table lying across his feet. His head was back and he moaned in pain. My mother kept saying, "It's all right now, Johnny, it's all right." She held his head against her legs as she knelt down beside him and we looked down at him as he gazed out in pain. His face was white, and there was blood on the floor.

He had fallen from the bed, and the heavy night table had crushed his foot. He tried to stifle the moans, and I could see him swallow. His huge chest rose and fell with the long breaths. He tried to turn his head away as the tears came to his eyes and slowly made their way down his face. "It's all right, Johnny. It's all right," my mother said as she held his head. Then she lifted her eyes to Mary and she said quietly, "Go down and put on some water." Then she looked at Paul and she said, "Bring me the big towel," and he went over to the chest and got the towel and she wrapped it around his foot. She held it in place with both hands.

His nightshirt had risen up over his thighs and I saw the whiteness of his legs and the black hair on them, the dark brown color of the soles of his feet. I found myself looking at his cock. It looked sad and forlorn lying on its side nestling in the black pubic hair. I suddenly felt I shouldn't look and I turned my head away for fear the others would see me, but I brought it back again and it looked back at me, dark, brown, and melancholy. I couldn't take my eyes away.

"Jackie, go downstairs and keep the fire going," my mother told me. "Make sure there is plenty of coal in the kitchen." I lingered, and then Mary came up the stairs with the water. "We'll see if we can get him back into the bed," my mother said, and she motioned to Paul to put his arm under his shoulder. She took his other arm and they tried to lift him but he shook them both off. He strained and stood up on one foot, reaching behind him until he felt the bed, and then fell down into it. He lay back and gasped, and I could see the sweat on his forehead. He moaned again, closing his eyes. Mary held the water while my mother cleaned the wound. She touched it gently, and my father's lips were pulled back tightly. I went down the stairs and carried in more coal for the fire.

All through the night until I could fall asleep I heard my mother talking gently to my father. Paul was awake, too, but we didn't talk. His eyes were open and he was staring at the ceiling, his hands clasped behind his head.

My father's alarm went off as usual in the morning, and when I heard it I was sure he would not be going to work, that he had just forgotten to reset the alarm. But I heard the voices from the bedroom and then my mother pleading with him. "Johnny, you can't go in with that foot. My God you'll never get as far as Monkstown for the tram. O Johnny, for God's sake don't be so foolish." I heard him mumble his answer, then he was on the stairs on the way to the kitchen. I heard him make his way down slowly, taking one step at a time, my mother behind him begging him all the way down to stay home.

"I'm going and that's that," he said finally.

"He's mad," Paul said to me, and I looked over at him in the dark. He kept saying "He's mad" over and over. "He never listens. He believes he owes his life to the bakery. He can't afford to miss a day. They might think he isn't loyal." I heard the front door close, and he was gone into the dark of the morning, limping, making his way slowly down the road to Monkstown.

I awoke to a pounding on the front door. It was Joe Kiernan, the milkman. I ran to the window and saw his van outside the house. My father was sitting in the front seat. Joe was helping him out and then holding him as they came up the path. My father's boot was covered with blood and his head was hanging to the side. Joe carried him into the house and put him in the chair by the fire. He had gone as far as Monkstown, Joe told us. "And I found him holding onto the railing outside the church, and he wasn't able to move. Well Jesus I knew he wouldn't be drunk that hour of the morning and when I went over to him he was in such pain he could hardly talk. I'll tell you, Mrs. Guiney, I don't know where he got the strength to go as far as he did on that foot. Jesus he's a hard man. Bloody terrible man he is."

We were all standing in the kitchen looking at him sitting in the chair. He looked up at us and his eyes darted among us and then he spoke in an angry voice. "Don't you have any school today?" he said, and then my mother ushered us out of the kitchen and closed the door.

"I don't know how we'll manage at all. God if it isn't one thing it's another," my mother said. "There will be nothing in the house this Christmas. The times when these things happen." I listened to my mother and felt my heart go down to my boots as she took the last few shillings from her pocket and sent me down to buy my father his cigarettes. "He'll die if he can't have his few smokes," she said. He sat in bed smoking and reading, calling down orders, and we ran up and down the stairs to answer him, thrilled at his helplessness.

He heard us leave for school in the mornings, and when

we protested an instruction by my mother he would shout down the stairs to let us know that he was there. "Do what you are told now and don't talk back to your mother," he'd say. We learned to protest quietly, afraid now because of the ally she had up the stairs. She would nod toward his bedroom if we answered her too quickly, and often we spoke to her in whispers. He discovered his home and saw his family come and go, and we approached him timidly. He was embarrassed that he found us and that we found him.

Mary had to leave school, and she got a job in the nursing home. "I don't like her being there at all," my mother said, "but sure we couldn't manage without the few shillings she brings home," and from his bed my father said, "She won't be a skivvy. I won't let her run around for those auld ones down there in Monkstown." "Oh, she doesn't run around for anybody," my mother said, "and she's not a skivvy. She works for the head nurse." The nursing home was for the retired well-to-do. "Well, I'll not have her running around for them or anyone else either. Not for that crowd," he said.

Christmas came with my father still in bed, and there was little of anything to be had. The oranges that came in my stocking were only a disappointment. I walked with Mary to the six o'clock mass Christmas morning. It was still dark as we passed down the road to the convent chapel, and for a brief time there was a place in the sky where we could see the stars and a place where the darkness began to meet the morning light. There was a quiet luster, and we could hear other footsteps in the dark of the morning. The church was quiet as if it knew this was a Christmas we had to pass through. The flowers stood quietly on the altar and the priest moved silently among them, whispering the prayers to himself. The Christ child stared out from the manger with His arms outstretched toward Mary and Joseph, who looked down at Him patiently. All of the promise. The end and the beginning. It will be different. It will last forever. Everything is white. There isn't any snow but it is white inside the church. White and gold and green and red. Nobody is angry today.

The frost lasted long that morning and the avenue rang with the occasional voices of children playing. All the houses faced each other along the avenue, and in the center was the green where Tommy Roches heard the Banshee cry and the grass lay green and still and wet. The fog came, too, when the frost was gone. The damp trickled down the walls of the house and we sat and listened to the carols being sung on the radio. Dinner was over and the dishes were put away. The cake my mother made was gone, too. "It's the smallest cake I ever made," she said. "But there was nothing to be had. Please God we'll have a bigger one next year."

Toward evening we heard footsteps on the stairs. We looked at each other and knew it could only be father. My mother opened the kitchen door, and there he stood looking in at us. "I thought I'd come down for a while," he said, and he smiled. My mother stood aside and Paul jumped up from my father's chair. He sat down and stretched his legs out in front of him. He looked at us all as if he had performed a magic trick, and then he turned to my mother and said, "How about a cup of tea, Kelly?" It was good to have him in the kitchen again.

For as long as I could remember, Aunt Lill's picture hung in the living room. She was my father's sister and she was in the convent in England. We were awed that such a person was the sister of our father. She had gone straight into the convent from school and had never been out in the world. A letter came to say that she was coming home. "Well, she'll be home in the spring," my mother told us. "God how many years is it since she's been here?" She looked like St. Theresa in the picture and she had a sanctity that was beyond all of us. She never forgot our birthdays and she had become the chronicler of the comings and goings of the various branches of the family from Dublin to Liverpool. And now we were going to see her. The picture was going to come to life.

"Well, your father will have to behave himself while she's

here," my mother said. "And I'll have to paint the house." My father played no part in the preparations for the return of his sister. "Sure he couldn't hang a nail," my mother said. I held the paint for her while she stood on the ladder and painted the impossible corners of the ceiling. "Where there's a will there's a way," she said, and when she was finished she stood back and admired her work: "Oh, I'm very pleased with that." When my father came home in the evening he glanced around and smiled and shook his head. She was almost embarrassed to let him know that she had done it.

When Aunt Lill came, we went down to the mail boat to meet her. The early-morning light was on the water and the smoke from the mail boat hung in the sky. All the people leaned against the railing of the boat looking down at us, waving. They were home, from all the places, Birmingham and Manchester and London and Leeds. All the places where the war had been. Where the bombs had dropped.

Aunt Lill stepped down onto the pier and came toward us with her small jaunty steps and her smile that I could see from far away. She was so small. She moved from side to side and she carried a suitcase which was nearly as big as she was. My father hugged her and they kissed. Then my mother hugged her and I thought they would never let go of one another. "O Johnny, you haven't changed a bit," she said to my father, and then she turned and walked toward us. "And Mary and Paul. Look at you, you are as big as houses. Look at you. And this must be Jackie. O Johnny, he's the spit of you. God, Johnny, you'll never be dead while Jackie's alive. Does he have his father's temper?" she asked, turning to my mother. "Oh, he does indeed," my mother said, laughing. And then Aunt Lill reached into the big deep pocket of her habit, which seemed to reach down to her ankles, and pulled out a handkerchief. It was the biggest I had ever seen.

She buried her head in it and blew her nose and wiped the tears from her eyes. My mother put her arm around her shoulder, my father took her suitcase, and we walked down the pier to where the cabs were waiting.

Away we went up the Marine Road with Aunt Lill talking on, telling all the news of all the scattered aunts and uncles and nieces and nephews in the far off places. My father was different while she was visiting. He smiled and nodded when she spoke to him. "Yes, yes," he said all the time laughing, and Aunt Lill asked my mother if he was behaving himself. She wasn't like the picture in the living room. Her face was different. It was round and shiny, not the young angel who always stared down at us. Now she was a jolly little nun and I couldn't believe she was my father's sister. The people on the avenue called her the little nun, and she greeted everyone with a lovely smile. It was as though she knew them, and they smiled back at her.

She brought a strange smell to the house—the nuns' smell. It was candles and incense and carbolic all together and it came from the ancient secret known only to nuns. She called Paul Jackie and she called me Paul. She went to mass and communion every morning and when she came home she went up to her room and prayed for a long time in thanksgiving and my mother made her breakfast and when she came back down the stairs and went into the kitchen she said, "My God, Cathleen, you didn't make all that for me." My mother catered to her and no amount of protest by Aunt Lill could stop her. It was as if Aunt Lill were a child who needed watching all the time, and there was a fear that if she were left alone for an instant she wouldn't know how to manage.

In the evenings she waited for my father to come home. "Is Johnny late?" she would ask my mother. "Ah no, Lill," my mother would tell her. "He's not too late. He may have had to work overtime. He should be home any time now." One night when dinner was long over, my father careened into the kitchen with a great stagger that sent a chair flying. He steadied himself against the wall with his outstretched arm. Then he lifted his head and looked at us. "Will you excuse a gentleman for barging into your kitchen like this?" he said. He winked at us and then whispered loudly, "The door isn't as wide as it used to be." We laughed and he smiled back at us. Then my mother said, "Come on now, mister, and have your dinner."

"Oh, now," he said. He cocked his head to one side and looked at my mother. "Oh, be the hokey. 'Come on now and have your dinner,' she says. Well now, me darlin', after I have had a sit at the fire if one of those lazy galoots would get up and give a gentleman a seat . . . and after I feel a bit of heat and look at the results in the paper, you may serve my dinner."

Aunt Lill was smiling at him and she said, "Come now, Johnny. Be a good man and sit at the table and have your dinner. Come on now."

He bent before her and looked her in the eye. "Did you come all the way from England to tell me to have me dinner? Now, if you tell me that you came all the way from England to tell me to have me dinner I'll sit down and have it. Be God you won't even see it. But now on the other hand if you didn't come all the way to tell me to have me dinner then I'll just sit down at the fire and warm meself and read the paper. Will that suit all of ye? Would you all be at your ease now if that is what I do? Or is there any of you who might object to that?" He looked around at all of us and we turned away from his gaze and looked at the floor. My mother was at the stove and she raised her eyes to the ceiling and closed them. Her face was red. She looked at Aunt Lill and said, "Now don't pay any attention to him." She knew him well. "You have to give him his head."

He sat in his chair by the fire, lost in the paper. He was turning the pages looking for the race results. I could smell his breath, the smell of whiskey and porter, the smell he always had. Sometimes it frightened me, at other times it made me feel glad. It was part of the smell of the kitchen, along with the fire and the stews and the tea. He raised his head from the paper and looked at my mother. "Is that what you have to say? 'Don't pay any attention to him.' Is that all you have to say? But sure why should you? Why should any of you? Sure who am I but the auld fool gets up every morning and goes to work and when he comes home after having a few jars finds his family looking at him as if he was a thief or something." My mother raised her eyes again and ground her teeth, shaking her head. He lowered his head and put the paper aside. "And sure what else would you expect? None of them came in. Jesus, none of them," and he took the betting tickets from his pocket and threw them into the fire and stared in after them, his chin resting on his chest.

"And it's just as well anyway," Aunt Lill said to him. "Wasting your money on the horses."

"Ah sure what's a bet? They do come in the odd auld time," he said.

"Odd is right," my mother said. "Odd indeed. I don't remember the last time you had a winner. Wait now. Wait a minute. Was it before the war? I think it was before the war. Aye it was. That's right. You won four shillings. Of course it was worth more then." We all tittered and tried to hold back the laughter and then suddenly we were laughing loudly and my father was trying to hold in his own laughter with his head still on his chest but now bobbing up and down. Aunt Lill's head was thrown back and she laughed with us. My mother stood by the stove with her apron raised to her face, wiping her tears. "Come on now and have your dinner," she said to him, and he rose from the fire still smiling and sat at the table and she put the plate before him.

"Oh, sure he hasn't changed a bit," Aunt Lill said, shaking her head. "Not a bit."

"And sure why should I?" he said, turning around in his chair and looking at her. "What do I have to change? Will you tell me that now, sister? What do I have to change?"

"Oh, you were always the one, Johnny. Me and Jenny always running after you, pulling you away from things. You had your poor father driven mad. Mad indeed."

"Aye, and look where he put me. He didn't keep me very long. Artane. Put me in Artane, and Nellie Potter down there in Gortmore took me up to Dublin, and left me, and be Jesus, that was the end of it. Artane school for the homeless till I was apprenticed. And not one of them tried to stop her and me own father couldn't come to see me. And when he dies he leaves his fields to my cousins. That's a man for you. Never stood up for himself in his life. Let them take them away from him. His own bloody fields. And you and Jenny went off, too. Off like orphans to the convent in Loughrea. The two of you in Loughrea and me in Artane. The family gone. And bloody Nellie Potter behind it all. She telling him what to do. Jesus he never came to see me once. The job always came first for him."

He stared into the paper and Aunt Lill looked at the back of his head. He chewed his food on his gums and held his knife and fork upright like daggers clenched in his fists. My mother looked imploringly at Aunt Lill, hoping she wouldn't talk back to him.

"Ah now, Johnny," Aunt Lill said. "There's not many like

Aunt Nellie. Not many at all. The best in the world she was to us. I don't know why you talk about her the way you do. She was only doing what any decent woman would do when our mother died."

"Send us away is what she did, and not a word from our father. Where was he? First he lets us go and then the fields."

He turned back to the paper. Then he turned around slowly and looked at her with a bitter grin. He shook his head and then turned back to the table again. "Give us a cup of tea, Kelly," he said to my mother, and she brought the pot to the table and poured him his tea. She glanced at him with love and anxiety on her face, trying to convey to him with a look all she felt for him. He nodded, still looking straight into the paper. We looked at Lill's face and knew she was thinking of more to say to him.

"And is the food getting any better over there, Lill?" my mother asked her. "Is there still the long queues at the shops? I hear it's impossible to get a piece of bacon." My mother looked at her as she spoke, hoping to divert her.

"Oh, it's getting better, Cathleen, but it's still very bad. My God, when I see the food here and smell the bacon in the mornings I see how blessed you are. God takes care of his own. Ah but some people never know when they are being given a gift.

"And Johnny, let me tell you, Jenny and myself were glad to go to Loughrea. Aye, and Jenny would tell you the same and look at her now in America doing so well. Working for the best families. God took care of his own. We have no need to fear. No indeed. Nothing to fear. Sure didn't we all turn out grand. All those girls from Loughrea that went to America and all found husbands and now all with families of their own. And don't I hear from them all. We have our own little family even if it's spread all over the world. Lovely families and good husbands. Not a bad one among them. God is good to his own. And look at your own cousins down there in Gortmore. The best in the world. Hardworking. Oh, I can't wait to go down and see them all.

"O Johnny, it would be nice for the two of us to go down there. We would see all the old crowd. Will you come down with me?" she asked him.

"I can't, Lill," my father said. "And to tell you the truth I wouldn't go even if I could. And as far as I'm concerned they won't see me in Gortmore till that crowd of them down there are long gone out of it."

Aunt Lill looked at him with shock on her face. She looked quickly at my mother and my mother half smiled and turned away to the stove. "Ah now, Johnny. You that grew up with them all. What's the matter? Will you tell me what's the matter?"

"Ask Joe Gormley when you go down there," he said. "Just ask him who owned all that land in back of Aunt Nellie's house and who owns it now. And ask him how they got it."

"O Johnny, you must be romancing. You must be romancing," she said, looking at him. "Who owned it? Who owned that land in back of Aunt Nellie's house?"

"Your own father owned it." He stared at her. "Your own father owned it and now they have it because they brought him the deeds when he was nearly dead and they had him sign them. That's the Gortmore crowd for you. Oh, I'm sure you'll find them all nice and they'll throw their houses open to you but sure why shouldn't they. Be Jesus it's the least they could do."

It was decided that I would go to Gortmore with Aunt Lill. I had never been away from home before, and Aunt Lill kept saying, "O Jackie, wait till you see Gortmore." It felt strange to be going there after the way my father spoke about his cousins. He didn't want me to go, but my mother said that Aunt Lill had to have someone to travel with her, and then he didn't say anything.

The village was so small standing on the top of a hill with a river flowing at the bottom. It stood very quietly with hardly a sound and the hill reached gently up to the sky that seemed to shield it. So quiet. I wondered where everyone was. Aunt Lill stopped at the house where my father was born.

"That was your grandfather's house," she said, and I looked. There was an iron gate standing between two tall pillars and a path leading up to a red door with a large black knocker on it. The house stood even more silent than the village, as though so much had passed it, and it looked sad and lonely and far away from its own time. The windows stared out like sad eyes, holding back, still not seeing. And then we came to a small shop with a sign over it that said Guiney, Baker and Grocer. The cousins owned it, Aunt Lill told me, and then we came to their house where we were going to stay.

"Come in. Come in," Aunt Cissy said when she opened the door. "My God, Lill, you're back. You look marvelous. Oh, thank God you're here. Michael, Michael, Lill is here."

And then a man came to the door, his face still wet, and he was wiping it with a towel and his suspenders were hanging down at his sides. He smiled when he saw Aunt Lill. "O Lill, Lill, my God you're here!" He beamed, his face still glistening from the water. "Come in. Come in." And then we were sitting in the living room. "And is that Johnny's lad?" he asked, looking at me. Aunt Lill nodded. "My God his father will never be dead while he's alive," he said. "He's the spit of Johnny. He'll have the girls after him like his father. Will you ever forget the way they used to run after Johnny?" They laughed and Aunt Cissy reached and ran her head through my hair. They were nice and I liked them. I remembered what my father had said about them that night in the kitchen.

Aunt Cissy made tea and we sat by the fire. They spoke of people and places I had never heard of and I was far away from them. I felt close to my father with a strange loyalty I had never known, and I suddenly felt that I wanted to be home. I didn't want to stay there. I was surrounded by another time which my father had moved away from, and even though I didn't understand it I could feel the embers, as if so much of the past was still in the air. My grandfather had died in this house. They said he had become very bad toward the end and they brought him to their house because someone had to be with him all the time. And then that night I slept in the bed where he died.

I lay in the dark afraid to sleep, wanting to be home. The sheets were cold. I lay in the darkness with my arms clasped around me, clinging to myself for fear that something I didn't understand would take me away. I wanted to be home, away from the place. They were nice, yes, but the feeling I had. The night was out through the window, black and silent, holding vapors, remnants of the past. I could feel myself sink into the bed and I wondered if these were the sheets my grandfather had died on. I rose and fell on waves of darkness and when I listened I could hear them talking through the door. I was glad to hear the voices to know they were still there.

"You know, Michael," I could hear Aunt Lill say, "Johnny never changed. He still has that terrible thing about his father. I never really knew how awful it was. I know they never said much to each other. They would just pass each other, and Johnny still blames him for putting him into Artane. Would you believe it, Michael, after all these years he still harps on that. And then he was angry because he says his own father left his fields to you and Cissy. Joe Gormley told him that when his father was on his deathbed he signed the fields over to you. God, Michael, there's such a fury in him."

"Well, Lill," Michael said, "your father often said he'd leave the fields to us because he said he didn't see that Johnny would have any use for them being up there in Dublin. Sure you might as well have them, he'd say. He called for the pen himself. Nobody said a word to him. That bloody Gormley. Leave it to him to start trouble."

"Ah well, what can you expect from him?" Aunt Lill said. "Sure isn't Johnny worse for listening to him." There was a silence and all the words fell over me as I lay in the dark.

"Your father was a very sad man," Michael said.

"Aye, he was."

"Whether it was that he and Johnny only saw the back of each other did it to him I don't know. They never wrote each other a note or remembered a Christmas or anything. They say he never got over the passing of your mother. He was a lonely man. And I suppose you could say, Lill, he wasn't good at the graces. Locked up in himself and worked so hard all his life. I often saw him years ago when the old crowd would be here. O Lill, remember the way they used to gather around Johnny? There would be Johnny in the middle of the crowd and you could hear his voice and his laugh above the others and them all laughing with him and your father watching him, standing at the gate of the house. He could never get close to Johnny. And all he had was his work. And I can tell you, Lill, Johnny only came down to the funeral because he had to. He went off with Joe Gormley every night he was here. Whatever he sees in him is beyond me. A rare sort of bloody pagan. Drunk every night of the week, cursing outside the church calling for Father Coyne to leave. You never heard the like of it in your life. Blaming the priests for everything. You know, Lill, I offered Johnny money for the fields and he wouldn't take it. God, he spat on the ground when I offered it to him. Wouldn't take it. But he wasn't himself at all when he was here. When I offered him the money he looked at me funny, and then he would only shake his head."

I had my knees pulled up to my chin, and I could smell the camphor from the sheets. I was cold, and I couldn't get warm. A shiver ran through me. I wanted the morning to come and all darkness to go away. I heard the chairs being pulled back from the fire and then they were saying good night, and I heard the doors closing and then the house was silent. I wanted to be in my own house. I thought of all these strangers who knew my father and of our house and the kitchen and us all sitting around the fire. Something stirred in me for my father. I knew that something had been kept away from him, and even as I lay in the darkness I could see him standing before me with a distant, painful look on his face.

Aunt Nellie's house was at the top of a small road, away from all the other houses in the village. It stood on the top of the road looking down on the village as though it were keeping an eye on it. It had small windows with white curtains looking out silently, closed tightly. I went there with Aunt Lill, and Aunt Nellie greeted us at the door. She put her arms around Aunt Lill, closing her eyes and feeling the pleasure of her return. She smiled through her false teeth and when she spoke in her croaking voice I couldn't understand her. They held each other and patted each other on the back until I thought they would never part and Aunt Nellie made noises through her nose as if she were trying not to cry.

"And this is Jackie," Aunt Lill said, and Aunt Nellie was looking at me from head to toe with the smile gone from her face. I didn't know where to turn.

"Like the father," she said, turning away and leading us into the kitchen. She made us sit before the fire where the kettle was whistling, while she moved to the table, putting out a white tablecloth and cutting thin slices of bread, never stopping talking to Aunt Lill over her shoulder. Everything clattered and banged. She took long strides back and forth to the hearth, checking the kettle and always looking for something else. At last she poured the tea, watching it come out of the spout of the pot. She shouted when she spoke, and Aunt Lill and she seemed to be always saying things at the same time—"Yes . . . Yes . . ."—and nodding their heads as if they had a way of speaking all their own which nobody else could understand. Aunt Nellie hardly sat to have her tea. As I drank mine, she looked over my shoulder at the plate before me and took the bread from it and put it in my hand. "Eat that now," she shouted. Once she turned quickly and caught me looking at her, and she kept her eyes on me after that as Aunt Lill spoke.

"Oh, he's like the father all right," she said finally. "Like the father," and then she sighed. "And how is poor Cathleen?"

"Oh, she's grand," Aunt Lill told her. "My God, the way she keeps that house and looks after them."

"Well, God knows the poor woman has her hands full with the father," Aunt Nellie said. "And he's lucky to have her. God knows where he might be if it wasn't for his poor wife. He broke his poor father's heart. Poor lonely man. The poor soul worked until he couldn't stand."

Aunt Lill looked at her and shook her head and then looked at me and smiled and Aunt Nellie's voice rose again.

"Him and that fellow Gormley when he was down here for the funeral. My God, the pair of them were a disgrace. He didn't have a decent word for his poor father. Nor for me, either. Hardly give me the time of day. O Lill, if you saw the way he'd look at me. Same as he did when he was a lad. Oh, a terrible anger in him. And angrier still that Michael and Cissy got the fields. Wouldn't take the money poor Michael offered him. He'll never let the poor father rest. What in the name of God would he do with them anyway, and him up there in Dublin?"

"Well, he thinks they should have been left to him," Aunt Lill said. "After all, he was the only son."

"And why should they?" Aunt Nellie asked her. "And he couldn't give his own father a nod or the time of day. Oh, no. Wouldn't have been right at all. Michael Guiney has far better use for them."

Aunt Lill looked at me and smiled again. "Do you want to go out to the orchard, Jackie?" she said. I stood up and left the house, glad I didn't have to be there.

In the orchard I stood looking at the trees. Some of the old, gnarled trunks were whitened. The tall, weedy grass grew around them and I could see the back of the bakery through the leaves. The smell of the bread wafted into the orchard. The butterflies flitted around me and I could hear the drone of the flies. I could see the sky at the top of the hill hanging down and then I sat under an old tree and I knew I was by myself. I wanted to see my father walking through the gate or hear his voice from the bakery.

I was counting the days to when we would go back to

Dublin. I didn't like sleeping in that bed, and each night I could hear the voices coming from the kitchen. I held the pillow to my ears so I couldn't hear them and I closed my eyes so I couldn't see the darkness. In the daylight I moved around the house hoping they wouldn't see me, joyless, conscious of my father. Something in me knew a dread, like a shame that set us apart. I felt it for all of us, and still never did I want so much to be with my own family, safe from the dread I could feel in the air of the place.

On the evening before I left all the relatives gathered at Michael and Cissy's. Aunt Nellie came for tea and Cissy baked all day. She took down her small, delicate teacups the color of duck eggs, so thin. She poured the tea from the matching pot and everyone sat and smiled, talking with Aunt Nellie, who shouted her replies and her questions.

On the wall there was an oval-framed picture of my grandparents when they were young. He stood at a table, with his hand resting on a book. His wife sat beside him in a dark dress, a sad, faraway look in her eyes and her hands clasped together in her lap. I stared at them from the table, looking at their faces, and I wished I could ask them what was wrong. It was as though they had been forced to stand together, staring out, knowing that one day I would look at them and ask them.

They didn't have an answer. The woman looked like my father. She had his mouth and his eyes, and her hair was black like his, too, but my grandfather was like a stranger staring out, his mustache drooping down, his sad lips hardly visible underneath. His suit was rumpled as if he had found it in a heap, but what I remembered most of all were his eyes. They were frightened and confused, as if he didn't know where to turn. I didn't see my father in him at all.

Aunt Lill told the others about the girls who had been in the orphanage with her in Loughrea. She knew where they all were and who they were married to and all the children they had. They were her family. They had all turned out so well. She had letters from all of them telling her how wonderful it all was. She remembered the nuns who taught her and still wrote to them, too. Her angel's face looked out red and shiny, smiling at the world. My father's sister.

Michael looked at me occasionally and winked. Tomorrow I would be on the way home away from that room and the bed with the sheets that smelled of camphor. My family would all be waiting for me and we would all sit by the fire together. I would lie in my own bed waiting for Paul to come home.

The lamps were lit and Michael put more coal on the fire and they moved their chairs closer. They still talked endlessly, and I was glad I didn't hear my father's name. The words became as one sound to me, a listless drone.

It was then that I heard a voice singing in the night. The voice rose and went higher and then there was a pause. They all stopped talking and looked at each other and then Michael nodded toward the window and said, "It must be Joe Gormley."

The voice rose again with the song. It stretched all the notes, rising and falling on the wind, and then it began to come closer to the house. I could hear the slow faltering steps on the gravel of the road.

"My God, he gets worse," Aunt Nellie said and Michael and Cissy nodded. "What in the name of God is he doing here, Michael?"

"I'm sure he's just passing by," Michael said, glancing toward the window. "He'll be going on down the road. Sure by the sound of it he doesn't have a leg under him."

"Bloody troublemaker," Aunt Nellie said. "An awful man."

The voice and the steps came closer and then there was a

knock on the door. Aunt Nellie glanced at Michael in alarm and they all turned toward the door.

"Are you going to open it?" Aunt Nellie whispered, but Michael didn't turn. He stared at the door as if he might be able to make Joe Gormley go away. There was another knock, louder than before. Nellie looked at the door angrily, as if she wanted to hurl something toward it, and we could hear Joe Gormley humming a song to himself on the other side, his feet shifting on the ground. The door rattled again as he knocked and he started to sing louder.

"I'll stand here till the door is opened. You'll hear me sing all night. I only want to have a look at Johnny's lad. I want to have a look at the boy. I'll be no trouble at all. Ah, sure, Michael, it's only meself."

Michael nodded toward Aunt Nellie and then he moved to the door and opened it. Joe Gormley stood at the door, looking in. He was tall and red-faced, looking as if he slept in the fields. His cap was pushed onto the back of his head and over his colorless shirt he wore an old jacket that had long since lost its color. His throat was tanned and long like a road reaching down under his chin. He tottered where he stood, and for an instant I thought he would fall. Aunt Nellie kept her eyes on the fire as if he weren't in the house. Aunt Lill glanced timidly at him, then turned away again.

"That's a lovely fire," Joe said. He stood behind them and held his hands toward the warmth and rubbed them together. "I only wanted to see the lad. I knew he was here with sister Rose. Sure I had to see Johnny's lad. Sure I'm his uncle," and then he turned toward me, and he was smiling.

"Oh, that's Johnny, all right. Oh, there's a lot of Johnny in him. We were always together, your father and me, two peas in a pod. Nobody ran around here like the two of us. No indeed. We were happy till he went off to Artane. And the two sisters went off to Loughrea. Did you know that? Did your father ever tell you of Joe Gormley?"

I shook my head and still he kept his eyes on me, never taking them away. He spoke to me as if the others were not there, and at times he had to hold onto the back of one of the chairs so he wouldn't fall. It was as though he had come from nowhere and had nowhere to go, and as I looked at him I could smell the drink from him, and his wink was like my father's. There was a gentleness in his eyes. Why did they say all those things about him? He didn't seem to notice that the others had their backs to him. He swayed, holding onto a chair. Cissy was busy with the dishes and Michael glanced at him anxiously, hoping he might go away.

"I suppose all good things have to pass," Joe said. "I thought Johnny and me would never be done being young lads together. Aye, and we had all the fields to roam in, the world as big as we ever wanted it. Sure God, it was only like yesterday. I can't believe all the time has passed. I never would have believed it. And Johnny's own lad sitting before me as young as we used to be. Well now, you can't get back what you lost, can you?" He looked at the fire as though all the years were passing through him.

"What's your name?" he asked me. I told him and he nodded. "I declare to God he'll never be dead while you're alive. And you can tell him Joe Gormley said that. Aye, and you can tell him I never let anyone say a word against him either. He was always independent. He'd stoop to no one. Not your father. If you're half the man your father is you'll be all right."

Aunt Nellie suddenly turned around as if she had been burned by the fire. "Leave the boy alone," she said. "And who are you to come into this house and talk? Bloody drunkard is all you are and all you'll ever be and it's never done Johnny a bit of good to be around the likes of you. Coming in here and giving out to the boy. Leave him alone. It's bad enough as it is between his father and you."

Joe looked at her and his eyes closed and he bowed his head and said, "Bless me Father for I have sinned. We can't have children around here. What they want is priests to forgive them and baskets to pass around. No room for children. Put all the children away. Sure they'd only be under our feet. You better not stay here too long, Jackie, or she might put you in Artane, too. Aye, you might be in the way."

"Go away from here, you devil!"

Aunt Lill put her arm over Aunt Nellie's shoulder and tried to turn her away. She looked up at Joe, frightened.

When he saw her face, he lowered his head. "I beg your pardon, sister," he muttered and turned and walked slowly toward the door.

I lay awake that night listening to the calls and cries of the animals in the dark. The wind came softly past the window and the curtain moved, and I thought I heard steps on the gravel of the road. The wind came up in a gust and the curtains rose up high, and I thought I heard a voice. I shivered and pulled the covers up to my chin and the voice came back again. It was singing. It sailed on the wind for a long time. I couldn't hear the words. It was as though whoever was singing was saying the words to himself with only himself to hear them. I wondered if the others could hear it and I was surprised that I wasn't afraid.

Long after it had stopped I lay awake. I kept seeing Joe's eyes on me, and I thought of him and my father running through the fields together when they were boys. Now they were all grown up and all the things that happened were so far away. There was so much I knew and still so much I didn't know. It was all inside me, turning and telling me, showing me, and I didn't understand it at all. I knew all that would ever be in my life but I didn't tell myself what it was.

It was at the end of that summer that Paul got a job in Guinness's. He had taken the examination that spring, and Brother Mallon had prepared him for it. My mother was overjoyed when word came, and Mallon said he was very proud of him, and I envied him, too. He was going to start as a messenger in the brewery. Davin and Roe went to the secondary and Paul went to work. I would see them go past the house on their way to school. They wore the school scarf—red, black, and yellow—and they talked loudly and laughed. I often walked behind them in those mornings and I wanted Paul to be with them. I knew that if he were, they would be listening to him and asking him how he did the homework and he would take his pages out and show them.

My mother got Paul up early each morning, and I woke

up with him. He would lie next to me with his eyes open, staring at the ceiling, and then my mother would call him again. He would close his eyes and say, "All right, all right," and then he would stare and I'd pretend to be asleep. Sometimes he sat on the edge of the bed for a long time, looking down at the floor with his shoulders bent, not moving. And then my mother would call up the stairs, "Hurry up, Paul, you'll be late," and then he would move slowly and close the bedroom door behind him, and I'd hear her move back into the kitchen from the stairs.

She made him his breakfast each morning and she'd say, "Come now, come on. You'll have to be quick. Eat that now. God, you have hardly any time for a bite at all." He always ran down the path, slamming the front door behind him, and then I'd hear him running down the road. I listened till his steps were gone, and I hoped he wouldn't be late. On Fridays he brought his pay envelope home and handed it to my mother. He waited till she handed him his part and sometimes he made a face. Mary brought her pay home, too, from the nursing home, and then she got a job at Clery's and there was so much excitement about it. She got it through Aunt Nellie, who knew the manager, and my mother said, "Well, I'm glad you are out of that place down there. I'm only sorry you had to be there at all. But it didn't do you any harm. None at all, and the few shillings were a godsend. Never turn your nose up at anything."

Paul saved enough to buy a bicycle, and he told my mother it would allow him at least a half-hour's extra sleep each morning, but the rush became even greater because he left himself no time at all now, and each morning he pedaled furiously to the station to try to catch his train. I watched him through the window, standing on the pedals, pounding with panic and determination. We were told he was seen going down Monkstown Hill as if he carried a message that would save the world, and when he made the turns at the bend in the road his legs nearly touched the ground. The train could always be heard in the distance, approaching the station, and when he heard it he pedaled with even greater fury. When he reached the station he jumped off the bicycle and ran to the entrance, and the bicycle crashed into the wall and fell to the ground, where it lay until his return in the evening.

On one morning as he pedaled with his head down, looking neither to the right nor to the left, he was hit by a car at an intersection. The bicycle was nearly bent double, but Paul was unhurt, and that evening he carried the bicycle home and put it in the shed at the back of the house, where it lay never to be ridden again, still shiny and new, but bent in two. We couldn't imagine how he had escaped unhurt. My mother gave thanks to God that he couldn't ride the bicycle anymore. She said that accident was a gift from God. My father always looked at him curiously, but after the accident he would leave the kitchen when Paul came in. "That fellow is mad," he'd say.

Paul didn't pay any attention to anyone, and he came and went, always under the eye of my father, who pretended that he never saw him. They walked around each other, and sometimes they forgot and they would talk, and my father always reminded him of how lucky he was to have the job in Guinness's. "I hope the other fellow will do as well," he'd say. I always felt my stomach turn over when he said it, because I was afraid I wouldn't please him.

I used to spend hours kicking a tennis ball against the wall outside the house, dreaming of becoming a football star and playing for one of the big teams in England. That was the answer for me. I wouldn't have to take the exam or work in the brewery. I would play football and be a great star and play for Ireland, too. I wouldn't have to bother with anything else. Just play football.

"You have the toes kicked out of your shoes," my mother always told me. "I'll have to tell your father. I can't be bringing them to the shoemaker every week. Bloody football. You have us all driven mad." But nothing could stop me, and each time I kicked the ball my whole being went into it and the ball slammed against the wall and came flying back at me and I kicked it again. I would pick it up and squeeze it and bounce it and feel the life in it. I discovered, too, that I could run and jump high into the air and feel the grass like springs under my feet. It was my own secret that I carried with me. I would play football. That was the way for me, and when I ran in Sutton's Field I could leap so that I thought I could stand still in the air and never come back down again. I could go high over the others, even the bigger fellows. I could go high over them and look down and see them looking up at me, and I felt the power in my body. I was as light as a feather, and I could feel all the sureness and the expectation in my heart, and there was no boundary for me between heaven and earth.

At night when I lay in bed waiting for Paul to come home I felt the energy in my body, and I had to force myself to lie still. I could feel myself rising up out of the bed and floating up over the rooftops to the field and I could run with the ball at my feet and hear the crowd roaring. I took long deep breaths that made my chest rise up until I thought it would burst. I could hear the clock ticking in the hall downstairs and it reminded me that Paul wasn't home. Was it midnight yet? God let him come home soon. I lay with my eyes open, staring toward the end of the bed, and the feeling came. A new feeling. It was gentle and started in my back near the base of my spine, and it traveled to the front of me, and then went down my legs. I trembled and I was frightened. I wanted it to come again. I lay still, and I could hear my breathing, and it came. The same way, so warm and secret, and it took me with it. It came again and again, and I forgot that Paul wasn't home and I didn't hear the clock. It came to me like a gift and I didn't know what it was or how to start it or make it stop except to lie in bed and stare at the ceiling and think of how it felt before. Finally there was the wetness. It was warm and it jumped out of me. I reached to it with my hand and smelled the strange smell of it.

When I sat in school I thought of it. I looked at Mr. Martin and at all the others in the class and I had my secret. I couldn't talk about it and I wondered what it was that had happened to me. I wanted to be by myself. I stared in the mirror, and I looked for changes. Was there anything different about me? The secret was with me all the time, and I wanted the house to be empty. I wanted everyone to go out. I wanted to find all the secret places in the house, too. I wanted to look in Mary's dresser and to put my hand in among her things. To feel the silk in my hands. To hold them and look at them and wait for the feeling to come to me. All the world began to stare back at me.

I found the top of the bookcase in the living room. I reached my hand up and found the magazines that were my father's. I looked at them quickly, flying through the pages. Women in bathing suits looked at me with their smiles. When I held the patten for the priest as he gave out communion, I looked at the people's faces and saw the white wafers resting on their tongues, and I wondered if they knew there was a secret.

It was then that my family became strangers to me. I avoided them. I saw my father standing in front of the church one Sunday waiting to go in to mass. Before he could see me, I turned away and came back again after he had gone in. I wondered if he saw me. I didn't know why I had turned away, but as I saw him standing I was overcome with a feeling of shame. I couldn't look at him or have anyone know he was my father. When I felt him look at me across the kitchen I was sure he knew. When I saw his face there was a hurt defiance in it, an amazement as if we had just discovered we lived in the same house. He wanted to talk to me and I wanted to hear him but I was afraid of what he would say.

One evening I had a fight. Michael Lynch and I rolled in the mud of the field and the other boys were all around us cheering and shouting. Suddenly I was rolled over on my back, looking up at the faces, and there was my father looking down at me. I stared back at him in fear, and then Lynch turned his head and looked up and we both stood up and my father walked away.

He started to come home earlier from work. He would take my mother to the pictures in the evening. When they stayed home they sat quietly at the fire facing each other while my mother read her book and he read the paper. The house was very quiet.

In the spring my mother was happier in the mornings. There was a new tone in her voice. She seemed younger. My father rarely came home late now. When he walked into the house, she smiled and glanced at him as if she had only found him. She didn't say anything when he threw the betting tickets into the fire. All she wanted was that he be home and now he was. They moved away from us in their own way. When they passed down the avenue together, I stood at the gate and looked after them. My father walked on the outside, taking his strong, determined steps. They nodded and smiled to the neighbors and when they came home they sat and drank their tea together. Mary and I felt like outsiders when we walked in on them.

On those evenings I kicked the ball against the wall with

fury and desperation. The summer evening skies were blue and red and looked down on me. There were voices all around me, and I kicked in desperation, feeling the power within me, afraid I couldn't catch up to it. I rose with it, and when I looked at the sky the feeling soared with me and I reached a place I knew I had been before. I could stare into that place and feel it and smile inside myself. Something inside talked to me and prompted me. It was with me all the time, taking me over the mountains and across the sea to Manchester and Liverpool and Leeds, and I heard the crowds as they cheered, and the roar as I scored the goal. I saw the ball hitting the back of the net and then I turned and ran back to the center of the field and the others hugged me and slapped me on the back.

"You'll have the toes kicked out of your shoes," my mother said. "At that bloody ball day and night. I think you are mad altogether. There's more to it all than kicking a bloody ball against a wall. It won't get you a job when the time comes." When she said those things, I tried not to hear them. I knew I didn't want a job. There was a secret. There was a place. When I walked with the lads to the sea on summer evenings past Monkstown Castle and I saw the trees tall and green and silent, I knew there was a place. I kept it with me. It was like the spring tide when it rose up over the rocks and covered everything. The water lapped gently, running into places it hadn't been before. There were times I stood still, looking across to the horizon, and I stared at the place where the sea and the sky came together. No matter how loudly the voices around me rang out, I had that place.

There was a man who came to paint the outside of the house, and I sat with him each day. He was old and he moved slowly. There was no hurry in him. I knew he came from a place and a time when things were different, and he said he knew my grandfather. I sat with him each day and he told me the way things used to be and who all the great players were. He said he knew some of them, too.

"We used to come up here for rabbits," he said. "You wouldn't see a soul around here. Now look at it. All the children and all the houses. It's a strange thing. Where do they all come from? I didn't know there was this many children in Ireland. Where will they all go? They arses out of their trousers and not a thing here for them. Ah sure Jasus, it's always been the same. I had to go away meself. Aye, I did. Years ago. I went all over the world on the ships, and then I look around me and all I see is children. I think they are coming out of the ground. Look at them. All of a sudden I see nothing around me but children."

He pointed all around him while he spoke, and then he turned his eyes back to his brush. He made the long slow strokes easily and gently. He was far away when he painted. Sometimes when he talked, his eyes lit up and sparkled, but when he turned to follow the brush again, they narrowed into the old look.

My father had that narrow look, too, as if he had seen something. As if you could never touch him, even if you talked to him for a long time.

"And what are you going to do?" the old man asked me.

"I'm going to play football."

"Are you, now?" he said without turning his head. "Well you have to be awful good. Aye indeed. I've seen some of them and we all felt sure they would be stars over there in England and sure God they were back on the next boat. I don't know what it is. They get over there and something happens. Whether it's the air or the atmosphere or what I don't know."

He was quiet for a while and he painted slowly and followed the brush with his eyes. Without turning, he started to talk again. "And then there is the others. You see them and they come and go and they come back to the auld place after they have been away for a time and they think they have advanced, you know. Oh, they come back here looking for all the changes and wanting you to tell them all the changes you see in them and they think they know more than those they left behind. They come back and they laugh at so many things, because they have been away. When I was on the ships there wasn't a day that I didn't want to come back here. I never wanted to be in any of the places. Just to be back. Now when they come back, they think they have to put on a show. The only thing I can tell you is that you'll see it for yourself one day if you go away. Sure what is there here? And if you are any good at the football you'll go to England. Sure God knows where you might go. You could wind up in Africa. Be Jesus that would be a shock for you. The only white man for miles around."

He laughed and dipped the brush. "You never know where you might wind up, auld son. Sure there is little for you here. But you could be a baker like your father."

"He won't let me be a baker. He's the last. He said none of us would be a baker. It's too hard, he says."

"Sure you're still only in school. You have the brother in Guinness's, don't you? Now that's the thing. Get in there and you'll be set for life."

"I'd like to go to the secondary school," I said. "But I know I never will. My father won't let me go. He said he'd never let one of us go to the secondary and wear one of the scarves. He says they are all prigs there, choking on their scarves and wearing blazers, looking like bloody fools."

"Well, there is an awful lot of fools goes to school who

should never be there and there is an awful lot of bright lads never gets the chance. I don't know. I don't like the scarves and the blazers, either. There is something foreign about them. They don't belong here. I don't blame your father for that. Never mind. The world is a big place. Sure you haven't even started out yet. I remember talking to an auld fella years ago, and he says to me, 'You'll go away,' he says, 'and you'll be away for a long time, and then one day you'll see it. It will be on you and you'll wonder where you came from. And for a long time you won't see what you left behind you, but then you'll see it and then you'll know. Aye, indeed,' he told me. 'Harder going back than leaving.' "

He looked at me for an instant and then he turned away again and raised the brush. "You come back and it takes years. Oh, years. I wanted to come back for a long time, and I was always leaving where I was, and I was only moving farther away." He looked at me, and then he looked at the sky. The clouds were racing. The wind came blowing down the avenue, carrying old leaves and pieces of paper with it. They twirled in mad circles. A great gust hit the side of the house, and the papers and the leaves flew down the avenue crazily in a mad chase, not knowing where they were going. We closed our eyes till the gust had passed. Then it was gone and the evening quiet returned; the trees stood still again.

He began to get ready to leave, and he gathered his tools that lay around him. He rubbed turpentine into his hands. They came together lovingly, seeking each other in the old ritual, sure that there would be countless times when they would come together again.

"There are some things never change at all. That wind there when it comes down off the mountain—it's still the same and God, I've been looking after it for years. Same bloody wind. Always have to close my eyes to it. Aye, and if you went down there to the sea you'd see the same tide and it still comes into the harbor the same way. And the auld mail boat goes back and forth coming and going. Oh, the auld talk is different. I was thinking the same things when I was your age. I didn't know what it was I wanted. Be Jesus I think I wanted everything. Never mind, auld son, it will all come to you. Ah sure, I don't even know what I'm talking about. Listen, son, go and kick your ball and don't be listening to auld men like me. Get up to the field there and chase the ball. Sure you are not done being a youngster yet."

"Maguire and Brennan are going to the secondary," I told my mother. I looked at her quietly and with longing. She nodded and looked away. She picked up her knitting, and her fingers flew and the needles clicked.

"Will you not be standing there breaking my heart," she said. "For the love and honor of God, will you go out? Go up to the field and kick your ball. You'd think it was the end of the world."

At night I lay awake waiting for Paul to come home to tell him how badly I wanted to go. In the dark lying in the bed I could hear my heart. I knew I couldn't go and I felt a feeling rise up in me. What will I do? And always the snores of my father rang through the house. I could hear the hall clock ticking on. Tick tock, tick tock, never any change, on and on. The snores, too. My father doesn't know and doesn't care. "Look at me," I wanted to say to him. "Look at me, for God's sake, look at me. Look at me without that look in your eyes. Look at me, look at me. What is it I need to take with me?"

Then I could hear him say, "Ah, for God's sake will you stop it? You are not the only one who never went to the secondary. Oh, yes, indeed. Look at them. Look at them after all their years at the secondary. Wind up at a desk in an insurance company making nothing and looking half dead. Sure Jesus, don't I see them sitting silent in the pubs? In the lounge. Never see them sitting at the bar. All the appearances to keep up. You are better off, auld son. Better off."

I heard Paul's footsteps on the stairs, and I wiped my eyes with the sheet and turned to the wall. I couldn't stop the sobs. He came to the bedroom and sat on the edge of the bed, and then I heard his shoes fall to the floor. I could smell the pub smell, the same smell my father brought home with him. He belched and sighed. He sat for a long time not moving, and I turned my head quietly to look at him. He was staring out the window, looking off, hardly breathing. I wondered what he saw. I thought he had fallen asleep, but then there was another long sigh and he swallowed and whispered something to himself, and then he began to laugh softly.

The snores of my father went on and on, and I watched Paul as he turned his head toward the door and began to imitate my father. He began to make variations on the snore, going higher and lower, and then he doubled over and laughed to himself again. He couldn't hold it back nor keep it quiet, and it burst from him, high and shrill. He lit a cigarette, and I could see his face for an instant by the light of the match. He blew the smoke toward the open window and then hung his head down on his chest. He began to cough. He opened the window and flung the cigarette out into the night and then lay back on the bed. I could smell the pub smell even more now. Then he fell asleep. He never took his clothes off and his head was next to mine, and his snores filled the house with my father's. I looked past him to the window and I could see the dark and I felt the room moving, taking us with it.

I closed my eyes and Paul reached out with his arm and

it fell across my chest. I was glad he was home, but I was frightened for him. I wondered why he laughed the way he did. That strange laugh, more of a jeer and a mock, and the look he had in his eyes. He knew something and it was in the way he laughed. He had a way of looking down with great disdain. He was separate from us. We were all separate.

"What does he do out till all hours of the night?" my father asked. "There's not a night he's home, and you can't get him up in the morning. He's gone to hell altogether." My mother said the same things. She could only stare and listen in anguish when my father spoke of him. We were all frightened for him.

His friends didn't call at the house anymore. He left them behind, and when I saw Davin and Roe they asked me how he was. They were all still in school.

"There is a madness in him," my father said. "I don't know what the bloody hell is wrong with him." Paul laughed at us, and that strange smile rarely left his face. He avoided my father and acted as if he weren't there. They glanced at each other over the top of the newspaper, and if their eyes met they quickly turned from each other. When they were in the house together we walked around them, or sometimes we stayed between them. My mother always sighed when Paul left the house, and then she began to worry about when he would be home.

Through that summer the courtship of my mother and father continued. She was ready to go out long before he came home, and each night they went off for their walk, my mother smiling, holding his arm. The house was silent when they were gone. The evening sun shone in the living-room window. I sat and looked at the light the way it came, and there was a stillness. I followed the light with my eyes, back up to the blue sky with the red clouds hanging over the roofs. I could hear the shouts of children playing on the avenue, the hurley sticks clashing and the mad laughter and the dull, flat calls from crows in the trees in back of the house. It was the last light of the day, and I felt as if it should have gone long ago, and we were stealing it, or that perhaps it wouldn't go away at all. Perhaps there wouldn't be any night and the light would forget to go away. If the light stayed there wouldn't be a tomorrow. But the light shifted and lengthened and the shadows came. It always seemed to brighten for a while as if it would come back, but then, almost suddenly, it was gone. The laughter and the shouts died down and the mothers' voices cried out for the stragglers to come home, and then the crows were silent, too.

I was studying for the Guinness exam one night, and the papers were set out before me when I heard my parents' steps on the path. "That's a grand night," my father said as he came in the door. He saw me sitting in the living room and he looked in at me and he said, "Were you minding the house? How about a cup of tea, Kelly?" he said over his shoulder to my mother, and he winked at me. I smiled at him, surprised, and I watched him as he sniffed the air and rubbed his hands together. I could hear my mother filling the kettle.

"The other fella isn't home, I suppose?" he said, looking at me. I shook my head and looked past him to my mother, who was standing behind him.

"Where in the name of God he goes I don't know," he said. "I know he doesn't go to McHugh's or Loughlin's because I've asked them if they ever see him. He's bloody strange I'll tell you that," he said, turning to my mother.

"Oh, leave him alone, Johnny," she said, looking at him with her soft look. "He'll be all right. Let him be."

He looked at me again. "Come on, you, up to bed with

you. I hope you're studying hard for Guinness's. Up to bed with you now." I put my books away and said good night and went up the stairs.

I heard my mother putting the cups on the table and the tea being poured. There was the soft murmur of their voices as they spoke, rising and falling gently. They had their secrets, too. There were looks that took them back to another time that we didn't know about. The strangeness of them. How close they were and how far they had come together. They knew about each other, and they hid from us, and it was as though there was something they didn't want us to find out. I could hear my father's laugh, the soft laugh that rose up in him. I could imagine his face and his mouth with his teeth out. He took them out when he came home even before he took his boots off. They sat in a glass over the sink in the kitchen, smiling out at us. His face was so different without the teeth. It became small and its expressions were never equal to the words that came from it. With the teeth gone, the face was comical like a mask and the lips stretched like a clown's across his face. His head seemed so small and his brown eyes had a wildness. They were always the part of him that responded first. And there was the tiredness, too. He shrank when he was tired as if there were nothing left of him. An old sack.

The front gate opened, and then I heard the key in the door and I heard Paul's voice in the hall.

"Oh, you are up," he said.

"Well, you are early," my mother said.

"Well, I was just out walking and I thought I'd amble on home. It's such a lovely night."

"Will you have a cup of tea?" my mother asked him.

"Yes, please," Paul said. He was quieter, and I could tell he hadn't been drinking.

"Were you on the pier?" my father asked him.

"No."

I could hear the rustle of the newspaper pages being turned and then my father coughing.

"Don't stay up too late yourself," my mother said. "You'll be leaving the house like a madman again in the morning. You ought to give yourself a little time so you can have a decent breakfast and not be breaking your neck trying to get out."

Paul didn't say anything, and I was surprised. Then there was the quietness again. There was only the occasional sound of the cups being placed down on the saucers and the rustle of the paper.

"And how is the job now, anyway?" my father asked him.

"The same," Paul said.

"Still you're lucky. God, set for life in there. Best bloody job in Dublin and you don't have to slave like me. Always hard to get in there, too. Oh, lucky, all right. I was damn glad when you got that. I swore I'd never let any of you wind up in the bakery like me. I'd have you do anything but go in there. I hope the other fella does as well. I'd like to see him get in there, too."

The thought of the exam rose up in me and I was afraid.

"He was crying when I went up to bed the other night," I heard Paul say. "He was turned to the wall and he didn't think I knew." They were quiet again. I wished Paul hadn't told them.

"I know he has his heart set on going to the secondary," Paul said. "Couldn't he go? Couldn't we manage it? We could manage it now. All the other fellows are going, and he wants to go with them and be on the team with them and he is bloody good on the field and in the class, too. I'm stuck in Guinness's, but he doesn't have to be." I heard my father's chair scrape the floor.

"He's not going to that bloody secondary and that's that,"

he said. "Bloody lot of prigs that goes there. He'll do just as well in the brewery like you, and you, bloody fool that you are, don't know when you are well off. Christ I don't know what gets into you. The best bloody job in Dublin that most of them would give their eyeteeth for, but there you are as always up on your fucking soapbox. Do you know you are an awful bloody fool? I never told you that, did I? But Christ, I'm telling you. You are an awful bloody fool. And a madman into the bargain. What the hell do you know about what's best for him? You have never seen in Dublin what I see every day. Aye, and what I have seen for as long as I've been in it. More poor children with the arses out of their trousers than those that haven't and no shoes on their feet and rare the time they have something decent to eat. And if you think I'm wrong about the bakery, I'd have you ask any of them that work with me where they would have their sons work. And you could ask them, too, if they would rather have them work in the brewery or send them to the secondary. Stuck in Guinness's, he says. Stuck in Guinness's. You are a bigger bloody fool than I thought. Oh, be Jesus, I know you. Knocking around with Sweeney and McAuley. Bloody pair of them. A good pair, all right. Not a penny between them, nor the sign of one either, and they have all the answers. In the name of Jasus would you get out of that and not be minding about your brother. Christ you're so smart you don't know enough to go to bed at night so you can get up in time for work of a morning. Bloody big shot in the pubs. Be God, I've heard. Brilliant, they say he is, and the poetry rolling off his tongue. Sweeney and McAuley. You better be careful who gives you your praises. Some of them would do anything for a drink."

"Well Christ, maybe they give me what I never got from you," Paul screamed back at him. His voice was high, and it cracked in a sob. "You make all the choices for us. Deny us your own trade, and won't let us go to school, and then tell us what fools we are because we don't like it. I wonder who the madman is. Jesus Christ, the years you rolled in here drunk, and we all terrified of you. You'd kill us quick as look at us, and you worked and had the work when no one around here had work, and we were worse off than anyone. Me and the pubs, you say. We saw little of you. Jesus don't talk to me about pubs. You fuckin' lived in them. What the hell did we see of you? When we did you were half jarred. And you won't see much of me." There was a loud crash and I could hear the sound of the table being pushed and the cups and saucers hitting the floor and then my mother screamed.

"For Christ's sake, stop it. Stop it," she pleaded. I could hear the grunts and the straining as they fought, and then I heard my father say, "You fuckin' little bastard." Their feet scraped on the floor, and my mother screamed at them. I trembled and held my hands between my legs and closed my eyes and tried not to hear.

"I'll kill you," my father was shouting, and my mother was crying loudly and begging them to stop. O God, make them stop. I heard Mary's steps running up the path to the door and then she ran into the kitchen screaming.

"I could hear you all the way down on the road. All the lights in the houses are on. You are making a show of us. For God's sake stop it. Stop it." I could hear the scuffling and then it stopped.

My mother was crying and Mary was talking softly to her. I was the cause of it all. The kitchen door opened and I heard Paul's footsteps on the stairs. He came up slowly and as he came into the bedroom he was still breathing heavily. He sat on the edge of the bed, sobbing quietly to himself. I stared at him in the dark. I wanted to reach out and touch him but my mouth was dry and I couldn't move.

It was not long after that he went away. My mother begged him not to go. My father didn't say anything. They never spoke after that night in the kitchen. The mock and the jeer were gone from Paul, and he didn't smile. I wanted him to stay, but I knew he had to go for his own sake. He brought home an old suitcase one day he had bought second-hand, and he got himself a few things, and then he was ready to go.

He left one evening late in the summer. The sky was red for a long time and it seemed all the children on the avenue were out. The dogs were barking and there were shouts and the people were standing at the gates of the houses. They looked when Paul walked down the path with the suitcase. He wouldn't let any of us go with him, and we stood at the door. I followed him to the gate and he stopped for a while and looked at me and smiled. "Keep the bed warm for me," he said. He looked to the door where Mary and my mother were standing, and he lifted his arm and waved and then he was walking down the avenue. He looked so much like my father—the way he had of sticking his chest out when he walked, the same broad shoulders. I wondered where his friends were. Surely they knew he was leaving. I didn't see them. There was a game going on up in the field. I wanted to run after him, because I loved him so much in the way that we never told each other but we knew. He knew all the nights I waited for him to come home, and even when he was angry at me, I didn't care.

I watched him until he turned off the avenue, and then he was gone. The white curtain in the living-room window moved and I could see my father through it, staring out. When I came into the house he still stood staring, smoking his cigarette with his hand in his pocket. He stood there for a long time.

Mary and my mother sat in the kitchen drinking tea, and the house was quieter than it had ever been. My mother stared down into her cup, and her bottom lip trembled. She rested her head on her hand, and Mary reached across the table and touched her. We sat for a long time and then it was dark. My father never came into the kitchen. We heard him slowly going up the stairs and then the sound of his alarm clock being wound to wake him for work in the morning, and in a short time his snores filled the house.

Paul was gone to England. Across the channel. To London. "To hell with Guinness's," Paul had said. "Let them have it. Best job in Dublin. Jesus let them have it."

When I walked on the seafront after he was gone, I always looked out across the bay past Howth and thought of him. I remembered a day in the winter when I had walked with him and the storm came up over the bay. The waves were sending spray up over the road, and parts of it were flooded. They came roaring in, breaking over the pier, and Paul left me standing on the road and made his way down to the pier. I was afraid he would be washed away. He stood there with his hands in his pockets and that mad smile. He turned his head and looked back at me. I waved to him to come back, I was afraid that the waves would get him, but he stood there drenched and then he came back laughing and salty and wet and put his arm around my shoulder and we walked home together.

There was a grayness and a sadness in that time. The heavy, melancholy grayness hung over us, and we were linked to all the other times. We were a haunted house entirely inhabited by ghosts. Pearse, Connolly, Larkin, McBride, Emmett, Wolf Tone, Father Murphy from old Kilcormack, the Croppy Boy, endless battles lost. The doors were slammed on the ghosts but they came in through the windows and down the chimneys and we became ghosts ourselves and joined in the revelry and we were lost. We could hear the speeches and we saw Emmett beheaded and Connolly brought in on a wheelchair to be shot by a firing squad, and we drank to them and we loved them and we wanted in our melancholy to stay in the house. The party overflowed out of the windows and up the chimney and into the pubs, and in the black Guinness we saw our faces reflected and we drank up. We drank the black graceful flowing Guinness. We needed to give our souls some pride, to lift our heads and take our hands from our pockets. To stop the mail boat going to England. There was an anger that was lost and buried in the grayness. It came with the lifting of an eyebrow or a quick glance or the shifting of a chair. It was in the refusal to raise the head from a book or the newspaper. It was in the sharp tongues of the Christian Brothers at the school and in the faces of the mothers standing on the doorsteps nodding vehemently to each other. It was in the devoutness at the novenas with the heads turned up to the high altar in pleading. It was in the way my mother poked her fingers into her purse, looking for the money that wasn't there. It was in Irish regiments in battles won and lost all over the world and never for themselves. They took the passion out of Ireland with them and they left it all in far places, and then they came back and told stories. But in the houses there was no passion. Only small sharp outbursts that didn't allow or require tender reconciliation, but only increased the distance and the pain and the frustration.

I could catch the tender glances, too, the quick wink that covered them up, but the words were never said. I saw the pain in my father's face when he looked at me.

"What will we do with that fella?" he asked my mother. "What is going to become of him at all?" "Ah, he's all right, Johnny," my mother told him.

There was something about all the men. They were far away. Removed. They always looked to the distance, lost in themselves. They didn't stand on the roads and talk to each other. They nodded and they passed as if it would pain them to talk. They knew of one another, and they didn't need to say anything. It was the same for all of them. On the last night of the men's retreat I stood in the back of the church and watched and listened as they held their lighted candles to renounce the devil and all his works and pomps and they sang the hymn. I heard the deep resonance of their voices.

Jesus Lord, I ask for mercy,
Let me not implore in vain.
All my sins I now detest them,
Never will I sin again.

They worked and lived in the same place and walked the same roads and they never knew each other. They walked from the church and the dark night was full of their voices and they went to their homes strangers, each of them, prisoners condemned to walk under the gray skies in loneliness.

Resignation held them, and they moved between their families and the pubs and the church, and they looked at us growing up, seeing the exuberance and the expectations and the talents and ambitions. They told us to put them all aside. It's not what it seems. It's not what it seems at all, they said. Go easy. Go easy. Leave the world alone. It won't do you any good.

O my father, I saw you in the vision of my dream. You stood over my bed, and you said I was your father, and you cried, and your tears fell down on me. You searched for your mother. You ran to the place where the crumbling walls of the old castle stood, the stones as gray as the sky, but she was gone. And I saw your father looking at you, and then you looked at me.

I believed at that time that all the important things that could happen were in England or far away or in the past. What was there to happen in our place? There was the war and all the men who went to it, but it was far away. We didn't see it or hear it. We were always looking on at all the things that happened in other places. What could ever happen here?

There were always the same people who walked the roads, and they were always sure to be the same as they had ever been. There was a scholar from the university, Nicholas Ryan, tall and haunted, with his head shaven, perpetually drunk, riding his bicycle slowly up Monkstown Hill and greeting us all in Gaelic. He'd stop and stand, staring at us with that madness, laughing to himself as we struggled to hide our own laughter from him. He was so secret and so far away from us. He never emerged from his drunkenness and he laughed at us from his secret place, always saying words in Gaelic to himself.

There was the woman with the clubfoot and the red hair they said was the Virgin Mary. She wore black boots that were always shined brightly, and it seemed that she had only half of one foot when she limped down the avenue. I often wondered why she couldn't fix her foot if she was the Virgin. She went up the avenue to have tea with the Healeys, and when she walked back down the avenue, she carried her beads in her hand and walked past us with her red hair streaming behind her. Where did she come from and where did she go? How was it the Virgin Mary lived among us? She wasn't even pretty. I dared not believe that she wasn't the Virgin. When I looked at her face and she caught me, she stared back with a strange look as if she knew what I was thinking. Don't you believe I'm the Virgin, she seemed to say. Don't you believe I'm the mother of God? She smiled without opening her lips and stared at me as she passed. Did she know all the awful secrets?

Another woman wore her dead husband's army uniform and marched up and down the avenue calling out the marching cadence. She cried out to us as she passed, "Look sharp there, you. You're on parade." We always stopped and saluted her, and then we would look after her. We never laughed. It was said she had money and gave a lot to the poor.

And there was the little man who sat on the wheels. He was no more than three feet high. He moved about on an axle of two wheels with a seat on the axle and they said he was married. He moved himself along with his feet, and he looked wise, and people bent down to hear him talk. They listened with great respect. We stood back to let him pass and we were thrilled if he nodded.

I kept wanting to know about things, to find out about the world. Nobody ever told me. I wanted to sing and dance and play music and be in plays and race across the swamp to Monkstown Castle in the middle of the night to see if the Headless Horseman was really there. To rob the orchard by the graveyard and sneak into the locked-up church at midnight to see what moved on the altar. To be on Killiney Hill with Dorry and lie on the grass with her and look into her face and tell her I never wanted to leave. To ask her to show me the way. To take me away from all the things that frightened me and to show me how to pass the Guinness's exam.

They were sending me out and I didn't know where to go. Why was it that I didn't know all about the world? I should have just known it myself. Nobody should ever have to tell me. All the questions I had that I couldn't ask: They rose up in my chest and beat with my heart. There was something that was wanted of me.

I could sing and dance and tell a story and answer all the questions you could ask me. Even the ones I didn't know. At the Feis Competition when they had asked me to translate an English sentence into Gaelic I didn't know, I made it up. They gave me a certificate with my name in Gaelic on it. You could make anything up.

And the stories that came back from all the places the men had been—the radio and the papers told us all the things that were going on. They were all far away, but everyone was so sure of what it was. But I didn't know. It was all so far away it never came near us. There were only the stories and the people on the roads who never changed, and always the voices of the children on the avenue on the way home from school. The girls in their uniforms and the boys in theirs and the scarves hanging over their shoulders and the caps on their heads. The poorer ones in hand-me-downs all running and shouting, laughing, pushing, turning. The evening clouds high above them, the voices ringing out as if they had found something. The clouds came from the eternal place where there was no past and no present. There were times I felt I could see all the way back to the past. That it wasn't far away at all, the place where the clouds met the mountains. There was a sadness in them perhaps because they had to keep seeing the same things over and over again. Always passing the same people in the same places and nothing ever changed.

A letter came from Paul, and my mother nearly rose out of her chair when she read it. She smiled and stared at me in wonder as she told me he was coming home. My father only nodded and went on reading when he heard the news.

"Thank God," my mother said. "Thank God we'll get to see him. He might not even want to go back."

My father said, "You never can tell with that fella. I'll believe it when I see him walk in the door."

I was preparing to do the Guinness exam. Brother Mallon was getting us ready, and he took great pride in the success he had had in placing so many. He had prepared Paul, and he expected much of me. "Your brother should have gone to the secondary. Brilliant lad. If you are half as smart as him you'll do all right. I hear he left the brewery."

"Yes sir," I told him. "He went to London." He shook his head and turned away.

He had a stick, the wooden shaft of a golf club. The end was painted with red ink. He told us it was blood. We feared him, and the stick even more. Mallon knew of my fear of math and he took a special interest in me because of Paul. He was determined that I should have the same success, but I still couldn't make head or tail of algebra.

My mother said, "Wouldn't it be great if you got Guinness's." I wished that there was some other way to get there. There was only the exam.

Mallon, despite being a religious, was a practical man and did not look for miracles. He kept me after classes and tutored me in math. He gave me copies of the previous exams to take home with me. They had notes written all over them but they didn't mean anything to me. All those terrible symbols looked up at me, and something inside me told me it was no use. I went to bed each night anticipating the wrath of Mallon in the morning and I got up early and went to the seven o'clock mass and swore before God that I would do anything if He would let me pass. "Don't worry, auld son," my father used to say. "You'll pass and you'll get in there and you'll stay. You'll know a good thing when you have it. You won't be a bloody fool like the other fella."

Mallon went over the papers with me each morning. The fog of ineptness came over me each time we sat together, and then he became compassionate. "Just do your best, and you never know what might happen."

The mothers thought he was wonderful because he got the boys through. Their sons wouldn't wind up in England, the land of pagans across the sea. We would be set for life. "Set for bloody life," my father said. God, if I could get it. I wanted it for them. I just wanted it for them. And I began to believe I wanted it for myself, too.

My mother went to the novena each night. "I prayed hard for you," she told me when she returned. I wished she wouldn't pray so hard. I wondered if there was something that could happen, something that could make everybody smile and take away the exam. What could happen?

There was a play we had done in school about a young child that was stolen by the fairies, and it was never found. They searched and searched and they asked the fairies to bring the child back, but it was never seen again. Could they come through my window at night? In the morning I would wake up in a strange place and they would all be looking at me. I wouldn't be frightened and they would smile at me. I would be in that place where the clouds come from. Or maybe I could go to the woman we thought was the Virgin Mary. I could ask her to let me pass. She could see to it. She knew the secret, too. And Johnny Seery knew it. They knew the weight of all the past that was pressing down. This exam that there was to do—where did it come from? Who put it there? Was it there in 1916? Who makes them? And this place, the air and the clouds? The world.

Davy McQueen was killed by a train in Dalkey station. They said Audrey pushed him onto the tracks. It was said they were having an argument and he was running to get away from her. And they had been drinking. He went to cross the tracks to the other side of the platform and he didn't see the train coming.

He had come home from England to look for a job because they wanted to stay. Mrs. McQueen had been so happy.

There was to be an inquest, and Audrey's picture was in the paper. There was a picture of Dalkey station, too, showing the place where Davy went onto the tracks. Mrs. McQueen said Audrey possessed Davy and couldn't stand it when he decided to come home to live in Ireland.

Crowds went up to the station and stood on each side of the platform and looked across the tracks at each other, and when the train came out from Dublin more people got off, and somebody said it was a pity you couldn't charge admission to the station. The men stood outside the pubs and gazed up the hill at the crowds. There were crowds outside the McQueens' house, too, and the curtains were drawn. There was a policeman standing at the gate. None of the McQueens could go in or out of the house without the crowds looking after them.

One night Dorry McQueen came up to our house, and she was crying. My mother brought her into the kitchen and sat her by the fire and made her drink a cup of tea. Dorry sobbed and for a long time she couldn't talk at all. "Davy . . . Davy," she said to herself. When my father came home he put his arm around her and she put her head against his chest, and he held her like that, and he looked at us, and then he rocked her gently and her eyes were closed. He didn't seem like my father at all. When she was quiet, he beckoned to my mother, and she put her arm around Dorry, and my father drank a cup of tea.

Dorry was so pretty, and she was always the most fun. She said if it wasn't for all the old crowd that came and sat with them every night she didn't know how they would manage. And she said she was worried about her mother; with the inquest coming she was afraid her mother would go mad altogether. Mrs. McQueen said she was going to sit through it all and see that Audrey got her due. "Poor Audrey," Dorry said. "Poor Audrey."

Brother Mallon said it would do us all far better to work hard for the exam than to be worrying about what was happening in Dalkey. He told us not to read the papers. "Reading about that won't do you any good. Leave it where it belongs."

I wondered what would happen to Davy's accordion.

Would it just sit in its case? I saw his hands on the ivory keys, his blond curly hair and the look on his face when he was strapping it on. I kept seeing Davy's face and I could see him and Audrey going up the hill to the station. It was said that they were arguing all the way up the hill, and that she was running behind him crying. It was two o'clock in the afternoon and it was quiet. Not many saw them, but they said that Davy was going on ahead of Audrey and she wanted him to stop, and he kept walking up the hill and they said she even found a stone on the road to throw after him but he wouldn't stop. He kept walking up the hill. And it was all because she didn't want him to stay in Ireland, they said. They said she was afraid of Mrs. McQueen, and they said, too, she was afraid of his old girl friends.

He made up his mind to stay because he liked Dalkey so much, and Dorry said he was sick of Birmingham. There was a time when he was sure he would never want to live in Ireland again, but he had changed. And that was the sad part of it, my mother said. "All the time Mrs. McQueen and all the old crowd wanted him to come back and the fuss they used to make over him when he would come home for a visit, and then to think that he came for good and was killed by the train in Dalkey station."

"It would make you wonder," my father said. "There is no sense to any of it. It always happens to the best, too."

On the day of the inquest they lined up outside the town hall from early in the morning. On the way to school with the math papers tucked in my bag for Mallon, I saw the crowd walking along as if they were going to find some great thing in the middle of the town. It was like the Corpus Christi procession. The road was full of people. There was a heavy fog, and I could hear the voices so low as if they were all one voice and the footsteps all together and people stood at the gates of the houses along the road watching as the crowd marched by. Johnny Seery limped along, his hands joined behind his back, and the woman they said was the Blessed Virgin limped along on her clubfoot. The little man on the wheels rolled himself along and spoke to the men walking beside him, and Nicholas Ryan drunk and on his bicycle was still muttering to himself as he rode slowly along, not seeing anyone.

"It's what they love most in all the world," my mother had said. "Someone else's misfortune." Was it enough to bring everything to a stop, I thought. Could it stop the exam?

I never saw so many people on the road. We looked at them and wondered who they all were and where they came from. There were old men and old women all staring ahead. Their looks were hard, as if they had been through it many times before.

The fog got heavier and rolled in off the sea; the town hall was lost in it. All who could went in and the rest stood outside in rows across the Marine Road looking up at the windows. The foghorns sounded in the harbor. From the classroom I could usually see the tower of the town hall and the clock, but the fog had rolled around it. I heard the bells chime the half-hour the way they always did and it was as if they were annoyed. They had a funny clang, impatient and flat and not deep like the bells of the church.

The town was so quiet that morning. I could see the gray outside the classroom windows hiding everything, and Mallon didn't talk. We read quietly from our books.

Davy had been buried up in Dean's Grange cemetery and nobody ever saw him again after he was killed. There were some terrible descriptions of what the train had done to him. The coffin was never opened. Some said he was drinking a lot since he came home and it was said that the two of them were drunk that day, but my father said that Davy was never much of a drinker and it wouldn't be like him at all to be drunk.

Audrey was an only child, and my mother always said she had an elegance about her, "But God, she is so frail, a gust of wind would blow her away. Ah, but she is lovely though. There is something lovely about her. You can tell she needs a man like Davy."

She had a lovely face. Gentle and fair and her high cheeks that gave her the elegance and her mouth with her lips that always looked as if she wanted to say something. She wasn't like Dorry, who could be all the things she was in front of you. Sometimes for a joke she'd even lift her skirt up and put it down again quickly, but you wouldn't think she was bad.

"The poor girl," my father said. "How will she ever be able to live the rest of her life, and all the days she has to remember what happened? My God, how can she live with it? What a terrible thing to have to carry with you. Sure it's an agony for her. The best thing they could do is just let her go home with her parents and leave Dalkey behind her."

"Oh, isn't it a pity they have to have the inquest?" my mother said.

"Well, now, we don't really know what happened," my father said. "She might well have pushed him and not meant to have him hit by the train. I have no doubt she didn't intend to kill poor Davy. Sure wasn't she crazy about him? Mad about him. Ah but then when you are like that they say you do strange things."

"But surely she didn't want to kill him," my mother insisted. "No matter what, I don't believe she wanted to push him under the train. They were so het up in the fight I'm sure neither of them noticed it coming."

I had often stood on the steel footbridge that went over the tracks and watched the train coming with the white smoke puffing up, and when it passed under the bridge the smoke enveloped me and for an instant I couldn't tell where I was, and then it cleared again, and I looked down at the carriages passing by underneath. I hadn't done it since Davy died, because when I saw the train I thought of him and I saw the blood and I remembered when we put pennies on the tracks and how they looked after the train had passed over them.

I didn't believe that she pushed him. My father told us there were some people who said she was trying to stop him from jumping but we didn't believe that, either.

"Sure, what reason would Davy McQueen have to kill himself? For Christ's sake some people would say anything," my father said. "If you heard the half of what they say in the pubs. We'll all be better off when it's over. Nothing has been right since the whole bloody thing began. The weather has been off, and the bloody bus has been late every morning, and with all the bloody strangers in the town it's hard to get a good pint. You can't even get into Silk's anymore. Bloody lot of auld fellas I never saw in my life before sitting in there as if they'd never been anyplace else in their lives. We'll all be glad when it's over."

Each morning on the way to school the same crowd was on the road and the fog hardly lifted. Every day the town hall was full, and the crowds stood on the street outside, waiting. It seemed that every word that ever passed between Davy and Audrey was in the papers, and it even told of how they met in Birmingham and what they did and how they lived.

Audrey's mother and father came from England, and their picture was in the paper. He was a small man with glasses, and he wore a soft hat, and he looked sadly at the camera. His wife, who was small, stared at him because she didn't know where to look. They looked so sad and all by themselves.

"Poor creatures," my mother said. "My heart goes out to them. Poor decent people like ourselves. Wouldn't you wish it was all over for them."

Every morning Mallon looked at my homework, and he didn't see any improvement. He had stopped commenting now, and he just wrote on the papers and handed them back to me. His stick sat on the desk before us. He hadn't used it for a long time, but still when I looked at it I thought it was alive and that it could jump up by itself and threaten us. "You've seen them come and go," Mallon used to say to the stick. "All they do is come and go and you and me always stay." He would smile at the stick and then look at us.

"I'll be here," he'd say. "It doesn't matter what goes on. I'll be here. It doesn't matter what happens. They can have all the inquests they want. I'll be preparing you for the Guinness's exam, and there will be them that will get it, and the rest will be on the boats and God knows where else. You'll be all over, and when you are there, when you are in Birmingham where Davy McQueen lived, and you are among the smoke and the dirt of the factories, you can think that you might have studied a little harder and been able to stay in your own country. And you wouldn't be coming home to the scandals and have all the country knowing your business. You can live your own decent life with your own and you'll never have to step farther from where you were born and reared. No need to go halfway around the world like so many of them. You'll be far better off in your own place with your own people and your own religion and you won't be led astray like so many of the stories I've heard. You won't have to make a terrible confession on your deathbed.

"Oh, you hear it so many times. So many times. They only came to it on the way out. By the grace of God. Old men in the far-off places away from the church for years and then the time comes for them to go and it's then that they call the priest. Don't you think it would have been better for them to stay in their own place? And don't you think that they have thought back and wondered what it was they could have done to be able to stay? Could all of you look back and say that you honestly did your best? Could you really say to yourself, I couldn't have done any better? And these are the questions you'll always have to ask yourself. Could I have done better? Did I honestly do my best? Believe me, boys, you'll carry them with you wherever you go. You'll hear it always. You can ignore it if you like, but it won't leave you.

"And if you can honestly say that you did your best, then you can lift up your head and it won't make a difference where you wind up. If you can honestly say, all right, I did what I had to do, then no man can say a word about you. And, boys, the truth is that you can't all get into Guinness's, and you can't all stay. But if you have the chance—if you are given the chance to stay—then you owe it to yourselves and to your families to do the very best you can. Oh, there are those that can't wait to get out. To get over to London and Birmingham and God knows where else. Or even to America. And believe me, boys, it's not what you see in the pictures. Oh, no. Oh, no. In those places you really have to work for every penny. In those places time is money. No time to waste. No looking at a lovely day. No indeed. And don't be fooled by those you see that come home. Indeed, don't be fooled. You might see the fine clothes and they may be flashing the money but they won't tell you what they have to do to get it. No, boys . . . no. The thing to do is to make sure that you have done all you can to pass."

It seemed that for those days of the inquest the fog never

left. It was like when the carnival came, the way it always rained. No sooner was the great tent set up and everything in its place than the rain began.

"Wasn't it starting to be foggy on the day he was killed?" my father said. "The bloody train came out of the fog and its own smoke, and sure Jesus it was on him before he knew it."

They had all begun to ask what would happen to Audrey. "Sure, it's all a confusion," my mother said. "No one knows what happened. And sure how could they? Poor Audrey hasn't said a word at all since it happened: She must be near-demented. My God, the look of her in those pictures in the paper."

The people who said they saw them walk up the hill to the station were called and they told about her looking for a stone on the road and then throwing it after Davy. It was what they called passion. She was passionate, they said. Was it in a state of passion that she was seen running after him? And was it a state of passion she was in when she threw the stone at him? That is what they were asked. Was she crying? Did she speak or cry out? Did the man turn? People on the road above the station said they heard her screaming, and they said Davy just kept walking on.

"Isn't it a queer thing," my father said, "that at the time it happened there was hardly anybody around at all, and then all these people come out, and they have all heard and seen everything and they all have a story to tell."

Every day Mrs. McQueen sat in the town hall. The papers said she kept her eyes on Audrey all the time. They even had to change Audrey's place in the court, because she was so uncomfortable. Even when she moved, Mrs. McQueen kept glancing at her all the time, and they said her face never changed. It wasn't her old fierceness, and it wasn't anger or even sorrow. All her daughters and the old Sunday crowd sat around her in the court and they all looked at Audrey, too. It was just like when she sat in the living room with Davy on Sundays. The paper said she never looked in any direction at all and her mother and father sat near her, and they were looking at the side that Mrs. McQueen was on. They never talked at all. The paper said her father had made an attempt to talk to Mrs. McQueen but she turned away and he was left standing.

Every day the mother and father walked out of the court together to the little hotel down on the seafront where they were staying, and always some of the crowd followed them. The fog rolled in off the harbor and up across the train tracks to where the hotel stood looking out over the bay. The town was never so full, and it was as if all the world had come to us like a great machine to show us how it did things. They wrote things of us we never knew.

"They have a way of seeing things," my father said. "They look at things in a far different way than you or I. Sure this is nothing to them. They are only thinking of where they are going next. They know what to look for. It's not easy to put things over on them. Oh, they have seen far more than you or I will ever see."

There was a rumor that someone standing on the seafront late one night heard an accordion playing from across the water, and they were saying it was Davy's. They said you couldn't make out the tune, but the music was heard. Most people laughed when they heard the story. My mother was angry, and she said that some people would make up anything to get their names in the papers, that if the whole thing didn't end soon we would all go mad. Father Sheehan spoke from the pulpit and said that justice was God's and not ours and we shouldn't read the papers or pay any attention to what was going on.

"It won't do you any good at all. Those poor people are

to be pitied. Just pray for them. Just pray for them and leave them alone."

I wondered if the music could really be heard. If I stood down on the seafront in the middle of the night would I hear Davy's accordion? I was afraid to go by myself, so I decided to ask Maguire to go with me. We planned to sneak out one night. We wouldn't tell anyone and we would go and stand down by the mail-boat pier and listen for the music. The papers said someone had heard it, and my father shook his head and said he was surprised that they would even print a thing like that.

"I thought those fellows knew what they were doing," he said. "Can you imagine the poor McQueens reading that?"

And then one night after I had sat with the Guinness's papers in the kitchen, looking at them, with the ugly math symbols staring back at me, I picked them up and said good night and went up the stairs. I lay down with my clothes on till it was time to leave. I heard Maguire's whistle outside the window and I climbed out over the kitchen roof and came around to the front of the house and we started to walk to the town.

It was midnight, and we walked the way the crowd passed every day. The fog was not so heavy, but it was still around us. Davy had come back, they said, to torment Audrey. It was a sign for sure that she had pushed him.

"My God, Father Sheehan is right," my mother said. "We'll all be demented by the time this awful thing is over."

We passed the town hall and stopped and looked up at the windows. The whole town was asleep, and there was only the sound of the foghorns coming off the water and the lapping sound of the soft sleeping waves touching the edge of the pier. There was no wind; everything was still. The town hall stood looking out over the harbor, quiet, and it didn't seem to have anything to do with what went on inside it each day. The dampness of the fog dripped down the granite walls, and you could write your name in the moisture on the great oak doors. The lights from the pier moved sadly and reluctantly in their reflections on the black water of the harbor. The long, black hulk of the mail boat sat along the pier in a deep slumber.

There was no movement on the mail boat. Nothing moved at all. We stood on the pier staring out over the water. Across the bay we could see a light sadly trying to break through the fog and make itself known to us. We could barely see the sailboats in the water below us, their sails furled and tall masts swaying sadly. It was as if they knew what was happening in the town. The flat bells in the tower of the town hall struck the half-hour in that awful tone, which had no heart and didn't care, but only gave the time. We knew we shouldn't have come. We stood and looked at each other, and I wanted to run home to my bed and lie down and listen to my father snoring. The harbor and the town were before us now, and I felt that they knew we were there, and they would show us some awful thing. Out of the silence would come all the terrible secrets, and Davy McQueen would come strolling down the Marine Road with the moisture running down the keys of his accordion, and he would play and look at us and tell us all the terrible things. Why were there these terrible things to know? All the things in the face of Audrey, and I knew all the time she only wanted to love. I knew. She saw all the things that were never said. All the things my mother and father knew and her parents knew. All the things that were never said and then when the train came and Davy was gone they only looked at her and they never said what the real things were. Better left alone. All the world was better left alone. Leave the world alone.

I remembered looking down my mother's breasts when my knee was being dressed. Let me look down into that place again. I knew I couldn't see it anymore. It was gone. All over like a wedding. A long time ago now. I could play and kick and run and go out into the dark of the night now, and there was a longing in me that I would follow anywhere.

We listened for the sound of the accordion to come across the water, and Maguire looked at me as if he expected me to tell him that I could hear it. I couldn't hear anything, and I stared at him. I could see his face in the dark, and his blond hair was wet from the damp. For an instant I wanted to laugh at him. We both reached our arms out and held onto each other's shoulders and we laughed quietly with each other in our fright and tried to keep it back. We didn't want to make any sound. He looked at me with that look he had. We couldn't hold it back, and a loud cry of laughter broke from him and he stepped back from me and bent over, his head shaking. His laughter went out over the water and I joined him and the sounds came back to us. All of a sudden it was as if everything in the harbor were laughing with us. We couldn't stop and we reached out and held onto each other again. I felt as if it would go on forever and I knew I wanted to laugh at all of them. Did they know anything at all? We knew about them. We knew, and we laughed, and we looked up past the Marine Road to the town that was sleeping. I wanted to knock on all the doors and run away and watch them all looking out into the street. I wanted them to hear us laughing. What did they know, sitting in their houses? All with the same look which never changed. The way they came out of the retreat with their heads bent down, smoking their cigarettes. They can have their Guinness exam. Let them have it. And Mallon, too.

Between us we had a beautiful joyous thing, even in the midst of our fright. We knew and we laughed, still holding onto each other, and then he was looking at me. His face had changed. His eyes looked startled, and then the laughter was gone. He turned his head to the side, then he quickly looked at me again, and his mouth was open.

"Did you hear it?" he said. I looked at him and I shook my head.

"Listen," he said. "Listen," and I strained to hear in the silence with the laughter gone.

"Jesus," Maguire said, "Jesus, I heard it. Listen."

"Are you kidding me?"

"I'm not, I'm not. I swear to God, listen."

I turned my ear toward the water, and I strained to hear. Maguire still held onto me. And then I heard the faint strain of an accordion, and he held my shoulders even tighter. Oh, it was a radio on the mail boat or something. Or it's on a yacht, I thought, but then it got louder, and I recognized the tune. "Here Comes the Man with the Mandolin" it was. My mouth was dry and I held onto Maguire, too. We didn't know whether to stand or to run and we looked toward the water and looked out into the blackness. We could see nothing. There was only the music, and it came gently like the waves. It would stay and then retreat again. Just the way Davy played it. "Tiddly oom pom pom, tiddly oom pom pom. Here comes the man with the mandolin." He always played it so that all the crowd in the living room on a Sunday could sing it with him. I had never heard the song anywhere else but the McQueens'. Who else could play it like Davy?

We stared out into the blackness, not able to believe our ears. And yet we could hear it. So that I was only afraid of what I knew. Without a word Maguire broke from me and turned and ran up the Marine Road. He was gone before I was aware of it, and I turned and ran after him.

We didn't say a word on the way home. We sailed through

the blackness of the night with the fog still clinging to everything around us. It wouldn't go away, and we made our way through it hardly daring to look behind us. Nobody would ever believe us. They wouldn't even listen. Who would believe us? And even though we didn't say it, I knew we would never tell anyone we heard Davy McQueen's accordion coming across the water.

I climbed up over the kitchen roof and then lay down on the bed with my clothes on. I could still smell the sea and the fog on them, and I stared up at the ceiling through the blackness. Where did he come from? Did we really hear him? Is there a way for the dead to come back? Wasn't he buried up in Dean's Grange?

I went to sleep, and then I woke up quickly. I couldn't remember if it had been a dream or if it had really happened. But it had happened. I began to know that there were many things that could be. All the things that could be. Mallon would be waiting in the morning for the math papers. I knew he would look at me. I could see his face with the small round glasses looking at me, his brown eyes seeing me and then turning down again, as if they knew something about me, something he knew but wouldn't tell me. I hated that look. Did he know this world was not for some people? Did he know that I was one of those who would go away? Did he know that I was one of those old men who would lie down to die in a far-off place? Could he see all that was ahead of me? Could he see that I didn't know? Old dried-up Christian Brother living in that place with all the other brothers across the road from the Convent of Mercy. All of them in their black. The way they walked the roads and warned us. "Leave it all alone," they said. I could hear the Fogartys' new baby cry that night and it wouldn't stop. On and on it cried, and still my father snored and I could hear Mrs. Fogarty humming and softly singing. "Little Annie Rooney is my sweetheart," but still the baby wouldn't stop.

If Paul were home I would tell him what I heard, even though I knew he would laugh. He would think it was great that we went down to the harbor, but he would laugh in that way he had because I knew there was something that was gone from him. He laughed at everything now.

On the last day of the inquest they said Davy's death was accidental. Mrs. McQueen never said a word. Her face never changed. And yet there was a sadness in it. You could see it around her eyes: a lonely, frightened look you could only tell was there if you knew her.

Audrey walked down the steps between her mother and father. There was a picture of her leaving. I could see the pain in her face, and the strain of the inquest. Her eyes looked huge and confused. It was as though she didn't know where to turn or what to do next. This terrible thing had happened and taken her with it. She was like a child, bewildered, afraid, and Davy was gone. The crowd stood at the bottom of the steps looking up at her, and pictures were being taken. People were laughing, too. I heard my father say he couldn't understand them. She stood on the bottom step staring at them but not seeing them and then she ran and they tried to stop her. She ran down to the harbor and went over the railing into the water near the place where I had stood with Maguire. And the mad crowd ran after her, and they took pictures of her in the water. They got her out, though. Beardy Russell dove in after her and he brought her up. They took her away to a sanitorium. All the reporters went away and everything was the way it always was. Something had happened. "Enough to last for a while," my father said.

But there would be the Guinness exam, no matter what happened. Each day brought it closer. It wouldn't go away.

"What is there to be afraid of?" my father asked me. "What is it?" I still see them both looking at me. They saw something in me but they never told me what it was. They saw each other in me. I am them. "Just get the job in the brewery. You'll be better off."

A few weeks before the exam I went to the brewery for a physical. It was a huge place standing alongside the Liffey. There were smokestacks and old red brick buildings and huge mountains of casks. Great Clydesdales stood between the shafts of drays, waiting to be loaded. There was the air of security. As solid as Dublin itself. Gray Dublin security. Long gray days. Always the sad purple mountains looking down. The gray pressed down like the great weight of all time. A frightening, demanding gray with the smell of Guinness in it. All the fear I had ever known was in the gray of Dublin. Ancient imprisoned fear. The gray of the betrayers and the informers. The gray of the inaccessible Trinity College. The gray of uncertainty. The gray of disappointment. The gray of shame. The gray of my unknown anger. Vague resignation. Vague belief in the impossible. The vague possibility of passing the exam. In my heart I knew I wouldn't be passing up along the Liffey very often. But there was the possibility. You never know.

There was a group of us ready to have our bodies examined on that late September day. There was a lovely warm fire glowing in the room as we stood. They called our names and we were examined. For all the time we were in the brewery the warmness stayed with us. The pick of the young men of Dublin, all standing in the warmness of the lovely fire in the brewery. For a while I forgot that there was an exam to be passed. Could it be that just by seeing us all standing there like that, they had decided we were good enough? No need for these fellows to do the exam. A wonderful crop of fine young men. Oh, we can tell. They had treated us so well. How could they possibly turn us down? The illusion lasted through the day. I rushed home to tell my mother I had passed the physical. She smiled and looked at me. "Don't worry, you'll get it," she said.

Dorry was the only one to visit Audrey after they had taken her away. One day she came to our house and asked me to go with her. I took Mary's bicycle and we started on the road to the place which was off near the mountains.

The asylum was an old mansion surrounded by a mossy wall. The windows were barred, and we could see the sky reflected in them. It was as if the house were empty and lost, standing in the field by itself. The black crows flew around it, diving and pecking in disdain.

We stood before the big door, and Dorry rang the bell. She turned and smiled at me again to reassure me, and then the door opened and a woman dressed in dark green looked at us. "Ah yes," she said. She turned and we followed her. We walked down a long corridor past many doors. The house was quiet. There was only the sound of our steps on the flagstones. The woman stopped and opened a door with a large key. "You have visitors," she said into the room, and Audrey appeared and smiled as she put her face in Dorry's shoulder. Then she lifted her eyes. Her black hair was cut short and I stared at her.

The room was small and bare, with only the cot and the chair and a small table. Audrey wore a blue cotton dress that was straight and not fitted to her. Her legs were bare, and she wore heavy shoes with low heels. I remembered the way she had looked on the day they took her away.

She saw me staring. "It's not bad here at all," she said. "It's not bad at all. If I had you here with me it would be perfect." Dorry laughed and they looked at each other and I tried not to smile and my heart was beating faster. I wanted to reach out and touch them both.

Audrey looked happy. Her eyes were bright, as if she had come home. No sadness in her at all. I looked at her and thought her more bright than ever. Brighter even than when she used to sit on the couch next to Davy while he played. Could I ever tell her of the night I went with Maguire to the harbor and heard the music? What would she think of that? I hadn't even told Dorry.

They sat and chatted and Dorry told her all the news. She talked of the old crowd. John Boylan had gotten a bigger job in the civil service and Joe Tunney was going out with Maureen O'Neill. Dorry said they would never change. "In a way you don't miss a thing," she said, and Audrey nodded back as if she knew.

"Oh, I know, Dorry pet," she said. "I know that I could never please your mother and those Sundays with Davy and the crowd all sitting and staring and singing and they sat and sat and said the same things every Sunday and sang the same songs and the way Davy used to be when he had to leave and go back to Birmingham. I was always so happy to go back with Davy but he used to leave something behind. And the mad processions down to the harbor and Joe Tunney leading us all down like a circus parade and then I'd wait for Davy to go to the rail again and I'd watch the change come over him. It was like an eviction every time. We would have been better off if we were not so close to home. If we had of been in South Africa or Australia or America but God we were between England and Ireland and it maddened me. And your mother hating him going and hating me for taking him and the crowd pulling him. Poor Davy. He used to talk in that strong way he had, determined to make his own way, but I knew the fear in him. And he hated Birmingham, too, and he wanted so much to be in Dalkey but he could never be there, either. I knew him so well. I knew all his fears. All the things he was afraid of, all the things that made him happy, and I could tell things about him that he didn't even know himself. He trusted me. I knew that he could see beyond all the Sundays sitting in the house with the crowd playing the accordion. He could see beyond your mother and father. He knew of the places. Some days we could be there together. But then we would come back and that's when he would be afraid. It would start with his anger. His terrible anger. O God, to see him. To see this thing come up in him. Dalkey maddened him, too, and he would be lost. He didn't even know how to say it."

She hung her head and looked at her feet. She shivered in the chair, and we were silent. I could hear the crows, and I caught a glance of them in the sky out through the barred window, and the sun came in like an intruder. There didn't seem to be a place for it in the room. Audrey looked up at us, and her face was bright.

"But when he smiled, was there anything like it? Was there? God, no one smiled like Davy. No wonder they all came to the house every Sunday. Why wouldn't they come? He gave them what he didn't even know he had. All the things he could have done. He never knew where to turn for himself. Between your mother and them all pulling at him. And maybe I pulled at him too much myself. Maybe I should have let him be. I had so much love for him. And I would tell him it anywhere and show him it anywhere, I didn't care. I never heard anyone say it here. They never say

I love you. Nobody says it. It's as if it doesn't matter. They sing songs and they tell stories. That's the way it always is, and nobody says I love you. There are no hugs. They all turn their eyes away and they are all dying for it." She started to cry and she sat with her face held in her hands, sobbing gently to herself.

Dorry caught my eye for a moment. I wanted to go and I wanted to stay, and she smiled to reassure me. O Dorry. She would always be able to show she loved. Two women together who would always say they loved. I didn't know what it was, and I didn't know the name for it, but I could feel the power of it.

"Oh, the way he felt that day, Dorry," Audrey said, looking at her with her soft eyes. "I could have loved him right there on the platform. There was no one around. I didn't care. We were going to really go away. We wouldn't stay in Dalkey. He knew we couldn't stay.

"We had run up the hill to the station and I was chasing him and throwing stones after him and I wanted to pull him into a garden and make love to him, and then we were in the station together and he couldn't run away from me anymore. He was laughing into my face. I held onto him and he pushed me away, still playing the game." She stopped and stared at the two of us and turned her head away. "He tried to cross to the other side of the station. I didn't even hear the train coming. I was going to run across after him. And they said I pushed him."

Dorry nodded and reached out and took Audrey's hand. The room was bright with the sun. She stared at Dorry's hand in hers. "I haven't talked about it before," she said. "I don't know why. It doesn't matter. God, that inquest. What was I going to tell them? How could I tell them something that I can't believe myself? Will I wake up one morning and know that it didn't happen? Will I ever believe it? I keep seeing it over and over again. I couldn't even talk to my mother and father. Oh, God, anything not to keep seeing it. I have to keep telling myself that I love him. When I know I still have my love then it's better. But . . . Still, the madness of it. Poor Davy. Poor Davy."

She held Dorry's hand and she bent forward in her chair and put her arm around Dorry's shoulder. They sat in the silence with the sun shining into the room. "They say I'm insane," Audrey said. "And some days I want to believe them. Some days I think I am. It's hard sometimes not to believe them. And they treat me like a child. They say I'm harmless. I hear them talking. I'm harmless, they say." She looked at Dorry and smiled as if she had told her something funny, and then she shook her head. "But still it doesn't matter. I have Davy still. I'll always have him. It doesn't matter where I go or what happens to me."

She smiled at Dorry again and then she looked at me as if she had forgotten I was there. "O Jackie, poor Jackie, and the way I was going on and on." I looked at her and remembered the way she used to squeeze my hand. She beckoned me over to her and took my hand. She held it as if she would never let go.

"Isn't he handsome?" Dorry said. "My mother fell in love with him the first day she saw him. The day he was born next door to us. There he was looking up at all of us with his eyes wide open. Always the eye for the girls. Oh, he knew to go to the girls. You should see all the girls when I walk down the street with him. And look at the eyes of him. Did you ever see a pair of eyes like that? Oh, he has a bit of the devil in him for sure. I tell you, Audrey, this fella will be trouble for the girls. And you should hear him sing. Learns all the songs from the radio. Every song you could think of.

All the latest. Let me tell you, this fella isn't harmless, and neither are you. It's those old bitches that are harmless. They'll go on and on. They'll be here long after you are out of here."

We all laughed when she said that, and then Audrey said, "Come on now, Jackie, sing a song for us. Come on now. I want to hear that lovely voice you have. You have all the songs."

"He does," Dorry said. "His mother told me. Knows every song they sing on the radio."

"Come on." Audrey pulled me to her and gave me a hug. She let me go and I stood back and looked at them. They were smiling. I started to sing. The song came out of me easily and slowly, and I could feel my voice. I just put the words to it and I felt them and they were between Audrey and Dorry and me. There was only one place in the whole world and that was where we were, and I sang and the words were just the words of the song I heard on the radio.

When I fall in love
It will be forever, or I'll never fall in love.
In a restless world like this is,
Love is ended before it's begun . . .

I was smiling deep inside me. There was nothing else. Only my voice and the feeling I had and Audrey and Dorry looking at me. I was beginning to believe I could rise up and jump and touch everything in the world. I could have all the smiles that could ever be if I would always sing and let it all come from that place inside me. My voice could take me wherever I wanted to go and could open up for me all the places I would ever want to be. I could let myself come out and glide on my voice, showing myself to the world, trotting myself across its golden bridge. I would be happy and do all the things I wanted to do.

The song ended, the door opened, and there were women standing in their green dresses and they clapped and smiled. "Oh, he's grand," they said. "We rarely get a song in here." "I think we'll keep him," one of them said and they looked at me. I turned my head. Dorry and Audrey smiled back at them.

We looked at each other in the strange room. The light of the sun was changing as evening came on. There was no sound at all now coming through the window. "Well, you'll have to be leaving soon," Audrey said. Dorry nodded. "I'd love you to sing some more," Audrey said, smiling at me. "I know you have lots of songs. You'll have to come with Dorry the next time. Will you? O Dorry, bring him. I might even sing a song for you. You will come back, won't you, Jackie." "Yes," I said. "I will. I'll come back."

We said good-bye to her and walked down the long hall past all the doors. In the evening light I could see away across the fields. They lay green and peaceful for as far as I could see. The amber light was deepening. It had seen everything. All the times that had passed. It brought peace and silence. It quieted everything. Light for all time covering all, gone so quickly and then came the darkness as we turned toward home.

We were moving into November, and my mother could only think of Paul coming home. We had not heard from him since he first told us he was coming. We didn't know the day but we knew it wasn't too far off. The exam was coming closer, too. That was a date that was too well known to me. Mallon urged us on and told us what to look for.

"You only have one chance. It's up to each one of you to be ready. Really now, for your mothers and fathers. They'll be glad to see you settled in a job. You'll be off their minds. You'll be out into the world. Think now, boys. Dwell upon it now. All the preparation for one day. All I can tell you is that you better be ready. There is only one chance."

We looked at him, and he looked out over us with his thin steel-rimmed glasses and his dark curly hair. There was still a boyish look about him in his long black cassock with the black sash. I always felt he was just dressed up for something he really didn't want to do at all. Perhaps he would really have liked to be one of the old men he spoke about, lying in some far-off place on a bamboo litter surrounded by natives, with the drums beating, telling the world he was dying.

There was always the chalk on his fingers and on his cassock, too. He had a way of rubbing his hands together after he had finished writing on the blackboard. There was the terrible scratching sound of the chalk as he wrote his well-formed letters. He left the *t*'s uncrossed and the *i*'s undotted until he had finished the sentence, and then he moved over it as if he were decorating. When he was satisfied, he would turn around and look at us and then he would ask us questions in that tone of voice he used when he knew we didn't know.

There were times he forgot he was Brother Mallon and a smile came to his face. He would take off his glasses, wipe them with his enormous handkerchief, and then sit on the high stool with his feet barely touching the floor. The stories he could tell us when he forgot where he was, and the look that came over his face. Was there no way he could go back to that place he told us about? Run out the door and off down the country? Go on. We'll cheer for you. We'll run to the door and stare down the hall after you and we'll tell them all that you have gone. Gone back to your own place. Urging us on and you yourself wanting to be out of it. Go on, run. We'll all run after you. But he never did. The old look came back to his face and he put his glasses back on and turned to the blackboard again.

I wasn't going to the secondary. We all just moved away from the thought. Maguire was going and some of the others. A new time was coming. There was beginning to be an accumulation of time past. All the days with Paul. Following him home from school. The time we pulled the dead branches of the tree home for the fire after the storm. And all the nights waiting for my father to come home. It was changing. Slipping away. Something had not worked.

December was coming again, and we began to hear the annual cry of my mother—"The Christmas nearly on us!" We heard from Paul, too. "We'll all be together," she said, "we'll all have a lovely Christmas. Oh, the way they used to be. We'll have plenty of everything. A grand Christmas. The best. Wait till you see."

The exam came first. It wouldn't go away. The day of reckoning, Mallon called it.

"No more hiding. You'll go there and you will either pass or you will fail. And when it is over it will be too late to worry. Too late indeed. And then you'll have to live with yourselves. You will know what it is to regret."

"Ah, to hell with him," Joe Kavanaugh said when we were walking home on the day before the exam. "Regret, me arse," he said. "To hell with auld Mallon. To hell with all the brothers," he said. And then he laughed out loud and kicked a tin can as if it were Mallon. "To hell with Mallon," he yelled after the can, and then he charged down the road after it and we followed him. He threw his school bag high into the air, and his books and papers came raining down out of the sky and fell before him. He kicked at them. He still laughed loudly, and he looked around with his cheeks red and puffed out, and his crooked teeth looked as if they were dancing. He didn't care, and he never would care.

Oh, to be like him. To be like Joe Kavanaugh. The way

he fought them. The way he wouldn't put his hand out to be slapped. The way he had pushed Mallon away from him. The way all the brothers humored him, afraid that they, too, would be the victims of his temper. "Fuck off," he told them, and he would kick at them if they came near him. He didn't care about Guinness's. He wanted to work on the trawlers with his father. All the Kavanaughs were like that. They would shake their fists at anyone.

"Oh, they're a tough crowd," my father said, "auld stock from Ringsend."

We walked home together that evening, laughing. The exam was buried away deep inside me, and the fear was gone. We knocked at the doors of houses as we passed by them, and then we ran before they were opened, and we shouted back at the figures looking out into the evening. All the energy rose up in us. When we passed Sutton's Dairy we hurled stones through the windows of the stables, and we heard the glass breaking and the horses neighing and stomping in fright. We called out George Sutton's name.

"You auld bastard. Auld ballix," and then we heard him racing across the yard.

We doubled over in our laughter. It rang from us and we cried out all the curses we knew. The footsteps chased us down the road and voices screamed after us.

"Bloody bowsies. I know who you are. Don't think you haven't been seen."

"Fuck off," we called back, and still we laughed.

We fell in a heap on top of one another in a hollow in the Boley Woods. We could hear our breathing, and each time the laughter died down it rose up again. We climbed the trees in the dark and called out curses. We named all the brothers and we said all we thought of them in a long litany. We could see the lights of the houses. All the families snug, sitting down to their tea. All the leaves had long since left the trees and the wind made a whistling sound around us. We held onto the branches as if they were the masts of a schooner at sea. I was wild-eyed and lost, and I hoped I would never come back from where I was, shaking my fist the way Joe Kavanaugh did.

I opened my eyes and heard the sound of my mother's voice calling me.

"You'll be late," she said, and it came over me in an instant. This was the day.

"Eat that breakfast, now," she told me when I sat in the kitchen. "Are your shoes shined? Give yourself a good wash now before you leave. And do behind your ears. Be sure to take a clean handkerchief with you."

I wondered how all those things would help me pass the exam. If I could do the math it wouldn't matter if my ears were dirty.

"Neatness is important," she told me. "Look at your father. Always clean and neat. It will carry you a long way."

It won't help me pass the exam, I thought. I tried to delay leaving.

"Can I have another cup of tea?"

"Come on, now. You'll be late. You'll be late. They'll all be started before you. Sure none of you are like your father. God, when I think of him. Up at half past four every morning and never a day late in his life."

He should let me be a baker, I thought. I wouldn't care what time I had to get up.

I couldn't delay any longer. My mother came to the front door with me.

"I prayed very hard for you last night. If God has any mercy at all He'll hear me." She looked at me and then she smiled, the sweetness and the sadness and all the years showing in her face. The wisps of gray hair fell over her forehead, and she held her apron in her two hands in an unconscious gesture of eternal worry, rubbing them together as she looked at me. She knew how I felt. Always the odd chance that something could turn out all right.

"Off with you, now," she said. I walked down the path to the front gate. She stood at the door looking after me.

I sat upstairs on the bus and we rolled up Sutton's Hill and then we passed through Foxrock where the rich people lived. All the lovely red-tiled houses with the name of each one on the front gate. They were called Glengariff and Inishfree and Cooldreenagh. Where did all those names come from? We passed the dairy. It was called Tel-El-Kebir. Why was it called that? There was a painting in the front window of the dairy shop showing a battle in North Africa. Someone had fought there and called the dairy after the battle. Years ago. We passed the mountains, too, on the way to the city. They stood purple and silent with the scattered cottages reaching up the sides and the ploughed fields below them. Always so silent and full of magic. What lovely secrets they had. And we came into the city. There were the black-shawled women hawking fruit and the bedraggled newsboys calling out and the crowds. The Liffey oozed through and the smell rose like the gray of the city. Smell of Dublin's soul. I could smell the brewery as the bus moved up along the river. Something awful and something nice about it.

The Guinness barges moved down the river piled high with the lovely stuff. The hogsheads were the color of brick. Fat and pregnant. But they used to say it wasn't the same after it left Dublin. Being transported did something to it.

"Ah, you'll never have a pint anywhere that will taste like

a pint in Dublin." Paul said that. "It doesn't matter where you go. It will never taste the same."

We were seated in the examination hall, row after row of us. The young men of Dublin. All the mothers' sons. The exam papers were laid out on the desks, facing down. Pencils and pens had been provided. Lovely long-nibbed pens and smartly sharpened pencils. At five minutes to nine a well-dressed gentleman came into the hall and stood before us.

"Good morning," he said in his West Briton accent. "As you can see, the examination papers are on your desks. You have been provided with pens and pencils. The first subject is mathematics, and when I tell you, please turn the paper over and begin. You will have an hour and a half for mathematics." My heart leaped to my throat.

"I would suggest to you that you make yourselves as comfortable as possible and look over the test. If you see questions you can handle, do them right away. Don't spend too much time on any one question. There will be no talking and no noise of any kind. If you have a question raise your hand and I will try to help you. All right. You may begin."

Where? I looked at the paper. Bloody, vile thing. It might as well have been written in Hebrew. Math. An hour and a half to kill. I looked around the room and saw them all with their heads bent down, intent on the problems. Jesus, I hated them. Bloody smart bastards. Look at them. No problem at all for them. I tried to catch a glance at the fellow's paper on the left of me. Head over it, writing furiously. I couldn't see it. Bastard had it covered with his arms. The West Briton was sitting at a raised desk at the front of the hall, reading. Occasionally he would cast a glance over us.

Someone raised a hand. The West Briton nodded toward it.

"Yes," he said.

"In question six, sir, do you want the answer to the nearest penny?" Jesus, he's up to six already and I haven't even started.

"Let me see," said the West Briton. "Yes, the nearest penny."

"Thank you, sir," said the boy.

No doubt he had the job. Running home to his mother. "Ah Sheamus, you're great," she'd say. "Oh, you're your father's son."

I looked at the clock. It was standing still. I wanted to get up and leave. No use in staying. Have to put something on the paper, though. It was like walking through a swamp. I tried. I was working hard on the last problem when the West Briton stood up and said, "All right, gentlemen, pass your papers up."

Well, the worst was over. I had no trouble the rest of the way. English and Irish were easy for me. I did well in them, I thought. And then it was over. We all left the brewery and went home.

"Well, how did you do?" my mother asked me when I walked in the door.

"I think I did well."

"Do you think you got it?" she asked me, her eyes shining.

"Well, I think I have a very good chance." And I was really beginning to believe it. More novenas and more prayers and surely St. Patrick would intercede for me.

Hail Glorious Saint Patrick
Dear saint of our Isle
On us thy poor children
Bestow a sweet smile.

And Mary the Mother of God would help, too. She had a whole litany of selves. Our Lady of Fatima, Our Lady of Lourdes and all the far-flung places. She was going to convert Russia, too. And if she can do that then she can surely get me into Guinness's. Just to please my mother. And there was always St. Jude, the patron saint of hopeless cases. All the weeping mothers, all the sons looking out at the world.

It was the year of my mother's Christmas. She prepared for it as if it were to be the only one. She started to gather things early and she made all the cakes and six plum puddings and she was going to paint the house. There was not a day that she didn't talk of Paul coming home.

"I wonder what he'll look like," she said. "Oh, we'll fatten him up."

She lived for the day. Gathering. Extra flour and extra butter, eggs and raisins, sultanas and almonds for the icing. She never left the house that she didn't come back with a bag of something.

"It will be like before the war," she said. "A prewar Christmas. Only better. And please God you'll have word about the exam. Oh, just wait till you see. Wait till you see. God is good. He'll give it to us. Oh, it will be a Christmas like we never had. Wait till you see."

She was excited all the time. Her face was flushed, and she smiled. Nothing could put her off. She went out each morning to the ten o'clock mass carrying her shopping basket, marching down the hill to the church. She wanted to fix everything. She believed there was a way. There was a way for all to be well. She set out each day to find all she could to give us a lovely Christmas.

"A Christmas like we never had." Each evening after the tea things were put away she sat down with Mary and went over everything. She made lists for the next day's shopping, telling Mary what she had found that day.

"Larkin is holding a lovely ham for me, and Goggins and Dempsey's have the turkey put away for me. I couldn't decide on the turkey or the goose. I'd love the goose, too. I'm very tempted to get it."

She glanced quickly at my father but he didn't look up, and then she nodded to Mary as if to tell her she was going to get it anyway.

Each day after the postman came, I ran into the hall to see if there was a letter from the brewery. I was always relieved when it wasn't there. My mother always said, "Don't worry. It will come. Wait till you see."

I went to mass each morning and prayed. I loved the church early in the morning and the smell. On weekdays it was different from Sundays. Quieter. I knew that all the people were there in earnest. They all wanted something, too. All the heads bowed, bent forward, and the huge stained glass window over the altar looking down on us. There were three figures on the window. The Father, the Son, and the Holy Ghost. I liked the Holy Ghost the best. He was the odd one. He didn't belong with the other two. There was a quietness about Him. The Father was watching all the time to see if you did anything wrong, and the Son was crucified and hung on the cross and had that terrible look on his face. Death. He died for us. The way his head hung down on his breast. Sometimes He had a sulky look. Look what they did to me. I don't mind. I did it for all of you. There was the wound in his side with the water coming out of it because He shed his last drop of blood for us. And the way his feet were placed one on top of the other with the nail holding them in place. The saddest man who ever lived. Oh, the pity we had for Him. Did He ever smile? Suffer the little children to come unto me. There was a picture of Him surrounded by the children and they were all looking at Him with their eyes lifted up and He had his arms reaching out before Him, but He didn't smile. The tired somber look He had. As if He knew the cross was just around the corner.

I used to stay after the mass and do the stations of the cross. I walked along with Him all the way.

"We adore Thee, O Christ, and praise Thee because by Thy holy cross Thou has redeemed the world."

He fell three times and He met his mother and my prayer book told how painful it was for her, his sorrowful mother, to behold her beloved Son laden with the burden of the cross. What unspeakable pangs her most tender heart experienced, it said. How earnestly did she desire to die in place of Him. And He is stripped of his garments and nailed to the cross, and then He looks out over all of us and He dies. It was always the same. Never a day that it was different. His mother and Mary Magdalene take Him down every day and clean Him and put Him away and then He is ready again for the next day. I loved Him and I was in awe of Him but there was that awful sadness about Him. He cried out to his Father, "Save me from this hour," but nothing happened. His Father looked down, too, and the Holy Ghost perched there with the light coming out of Him. He sat with the golden halo around his small bird head and the light came out of Him in the shape of a cross. But nothing happened.

Did God know where the brewery was? Could He look down and see it? I was always looking up at Him, wondering if He knew. Wasn't He an old patriot, too, with his crown of thorns on his head? Epitaphs. Stories of the dead. The long line of dead rising up out of the graves. Staring at us like Jesus. Sulky pack of dead. Drunks living in our houses. Dead staring down at us. The dead would never die. Walking in the streets with us. The dead and the past holding on. Bow down to the dead.

One day my mother told me she had met Mrs. Kavanaugh coming out of mass. Mrs. Kavanaugh told her that Joe had gotten word that he had passed. He was to start in two weeks. Jesus, I thought. Those who have passed get the letters first. They must, or I would have gotten mine.

"Never mind, now," my mother told me. "You still have a chance. Look how long it took Paul to get word. Listen, we're not dead yet. Just keep praying to God. Keep going to mass. I bet you'll get it."

I met Joe Kavanaugh at the football field. He was all smiles when he walked over to me.

"Any word, Jackie?"

"Not yet. It must be great for you, Joe."

"Ah, my mother feels better about it than I do."

"And you start in two weeks?" He nodded.

"I hope you get it, too, Jackie. We can go in on the bus together every day."

"That would be great."

I kept going to mass every day. I thought of my father lying up in bed all those Sundays when he didn't go to mass. I wondered why he didn't go.

"Your father needs his rest," my mother used to tell us. "Never mind about your father, wait till you see him on Christmas Day. He'll stay for four masses. Aye, and he'll receive communion, too."

I had never known him to go to confession or communion. I never heard him mention God. He didn't seem like the other men. He used to jeer at the men who went running to the church all the time, and he had a special contempt for the ushers, those who took the collections and sold the Catholic papers.

"Did you ever see such a crowd in your life?" he'd say. "Jesus, they'd make you laugh. Not tuppence between them all. Ah they give me a pain in the arse. They all think they'll be in heaven before the rest of us. Well Jesus, let them think it. They'll be taking the collection up there, too. Bloody faces on them. Dogs in the manger. Looking down at the rest of us. Poor bloody bastards."

But still I wanted him to be more like them. I would have loved to have seen him standing at the back of the church or marching up the middle aisle on a Sunday to take up the collection. Maguire's father did and he was a nice man, too.

It was only for the half-hour of the mass every morning when the world was still that I could feel the closeness of the God I didn't know. He had a heart. All decent people have a heart. He knew. If He came to our house, we would give Him what we had.

Joe Kavanaugh started, and some mornings I saw him waiting for the bus with the regulars. He was important to the family now.

"Mrs. Kavanaugh is charmed," my mother told me. "Oh, there's a great change in her. She doesn't know herself. And wait till you see. You'll get it, too. God is good. Wait till you see."

Christmas was coming closer, and still my mother had not stopped her shopping. Paul was coming home and we were going to have the best Christmas ever.

"We have waited a long time," she said. "I haven't seen so much stuff in the shops since before the war," she told us.

Every time she came home she couldn't wait to go out again, as if she were afraid she would miss something. Even on those cold, damp December days the sweat ran down her face, and she looked so pleased when she put her shopping basket down on the kitchen table. She lined all the things up and counted them and stood back looking at them. She was always missing something. There was always something she forgot.

My father looked at her with a smile on his face. There was a strange peace in the house. It had never been there before. It was as though some long battle was over. The war was gone. All the men had come home and we didn't have to queue up at the shop anymore for my father's cigarettes. There were a lot of things we had that we didn't have before. But the peace in the house had nothing to do with them. It was with us in the evenings when my mother was still busy making cakes and darning socks or ironing clothes. It settled all around us like a stranger, and each day when the letter didn't come I knew the peace would be there that night waiting for us.

Everything led to the Christmas Day. Every breath, every morsel eaten, and all the words spoken were only a preparation for the day. It would be the beginning of all the endless laughter. There would never be another angry voice, and I wished I could make time stand still.

It was that week that my mother sent me to the bakery with my father's clean work clothes. In O'Connell Street the crowds moved on the sidewalks, and I clutched the brown paper parcel under my arm. The Dublin gray still hung down, but the crowds were laughing and happy and the windows of the shops were red and they glowed in the gray. The children held the colored parcels given them by Santa Claus. The turkeys hung with their heads down in the butchers' windows. We had ours, the first I could remember. I made my way to Store Street, past the hawkers and the pubs, and I knew it was my father's world. He knew it all so well. I passed through the gates into the yard of the bakery. O'Rourke's. I passed over the cobblestones where the horses stood between the shafts of the yellow bread vans, and even in the yard I could hear the noise from inside the bakery. I could see the shapes of the men through the windows. They were like phantoms, all in white, with the sweat glistening on their faces. I stared in and looked for my father but all the men looked the same. They moved in silence, feeding the ovens and kneading the bread with their great strong arms. When the doors of the ovens swung open, their faces glowed and their eyes stood out in the their heads and they stared back fiercely into the light of the ovens as the doors swung shut again. I could see the muscles on their arms, and their clothes were soaked through with sweat. The white dust from the flour clung to them, and they moved about like ghosts.

I passed through where a man sat at a desk.

"And what can I do for you?"

"I'm here to see Mr. Guiney."

"And are you Johnny Guiney's lad?" I nodded.

"Well let me tell you, there's no finer man than your father. Don't ever forget that. What's your name?"

"Jackie."

"Aye, indeed. You're a Guiney all right. Aye, and your father will never be dead while you're alive by the looks of it. And sure if you're half the man your father is you'll do all right. Come on, now. I'll show you where he is."

He walked down a long tiled passage, and then we passed under an arch. I could see the men and feel the blast of heat that rushed over me. The man called out loudly over the noise.

"Johnny. Johnny Guiney. The lad is here to see you." And then he turned to me. "There you are now."

I saw a figure walking toward me. It was dressed in white like all the other men. His face was white like a clown's and there were old boots with the tongues sticking out of them on his feet. He seemed small and frail and bent and his dark eyes looked at me with kindness and recognition. It was only when he stood before me that I knew it was my father.

"Hello, son," he said. "Did you bring the clean clothes with you?" He looked sad and kind and there was a cigarette stuck over his ear. "Stand there a minute now," he told me, and he walked back to the ovens and looked at a gauge. He opened the door to one of them, then with a long pole he moved the bread around.

He was not the man who sat in our kitchen every night. Was it his voice that brought terror to us? Was it his happiness was a relief to us? He was small. So small, and his huge shoulders were hunched as he bowed before the power of the ovens. He moved in the heat like a man condemned by a mad allegiance to the sweat of the bakery.

"There is no one like your father," the man had told me. "No one like your father." I saw the other men all around him in their whites. I swallowed and for an instant couldn't catch my breath. This is where he comes every day, I thought. The ovens were opened and the fresh bread came out on the large trays steaming and I could smell its powerful smell. It mingled with the smell of the sweat and the flour and the fire of the ovens. He was so small. His face almost lost in concentration. A baker making bread. That is what he did.

"Aye, and I'll be the last, too," he told us. "There'll be none of you in the bloody bakery, I don't care what happens. You are not coming in here."

Only he could be a baker. None of us would ever stand before the ovens as he did. I stood fascinated, watching all the men. I listened to the sound of their laughter as they joked among themselves. They bore the work in the same way they walked the roads. All the more lonely because of their camaraderie. Could they ever be united for the deep deep sadness inside them? They came together for unions and they went on strike and they drew the dole but they never came to each other from their hearts. Each held his own heart staunchly in place, keeping it from breaking apart by the sound of his laughter and the loneliness of his toil. There would always be a time that would redeem them. Another election. The Labour Party. When De Valera is gone. A united Ireland. When the children are all grown and have good jobs.

He placed the long pole against the wall and walked toward me.

"Come on with me, son. We'll go to the lockers."

I followed him down the red-tiled passageway, and he walked into a room and sat on a long bench. The sweat glistened on his face.

"Well, how are you, auld son?" I felt so close to him. He lifted his head and looked at me with his eyes shining.

"Grand," I said, and he reached out for the parcel. He stood and opened his locker and placed the parcel on the bench.

"Jasus, I really need these. When the flour gets into them they hold the sweat and you might as well be wearing a wet blanket." He opened the parcel and took out the singlet and then he took the dirty one off and I could see his chest. It was pure white as though it had never seen the sun and there was a cluster of curly gray hair in the center of it like an island. I could see the muscles on his arms. They were like a boxer's, thick and solid and strong. When he leaned back to pull the clean singlet over his head, I could see the full expanse of his chest, so broad it threatened to push through the fabric. When he released his breath his shoulders were hunched again in an old resignation, as if they knew he had to go back to the ovens. He pulled his white trousers down quickly and I could see that he wore no underwear. In an instant the clean ones were on him and he took a towel from the locker and held it to his face and then rubbed it over the back of his neck. He turned to me and smiled and then hung the towel back inside the locker.

"Ah sure it's a hard life, auld son. But I suppose there is worse. But all the same I'd never want you working in here. Sure it's no life, son. Just wait till you see. You'll get word from the brewery and you can start in there and not be a fool like your brother. You'll stay there. Sure Jesus, it's the best job in Dublin. No matter what, son, you're not coming in here. I'd have you walk the roads first. Ah, no, son, I wouldn't want you working like this. Your poor mother wouldn't like it, either. Sure it would break her heart. She has her heart set on you working in the brewery. That would give her the best Christmas of all. Never mind, son, it'll all be gameball."

And then he reached into his locker again and turned to me and pressed a half-crown into my hand and he said, "Now don't tell your mother I gave you that." His brown eyes looked at me and I didn't know what to say to him. "I have to go back now, son. Go on home now." He closed the locker, and I followed him out to the corridor.

"Good-bye now," he said to me, and he turned and walked down the hall toward the ovens. His boots were white from the dust, and they dragged on the tiles of the floor. I could see the back of his head. His tough, fierce head. He could raise it in anger, but now it was bowed as he passed under the arch and then he was gone.

I walked back over the cobblestones of the yard and I felt the half-crown in my pocket. I held it tightly with my fist wrapped around it; it burned as if it had come from the ovens. I passed by the hawkers again in Henry Street, the old shawled women and the young ones shawled, too, as they called out into the gray air. The stained-glass doors of the pubs opened and closed and the voices rose in the gray, the long long lament of the endless striving. Profane and shameless. They knew who I was. They could tell. They knew everything. Another race. Not frightened of priests or exams or jobs. They sold their oranges and the vegetables and the fish with their babies in prams alongside the wicker carts. My father said they were the salt of the earth. The best in the world.

I passed into O'Connell Street, and I saw the college boys and the girls in their scarves and blazers, their voices rising into the gray. Their accents were different. They jostled and pulled at each other's caps and they laughed with all the right of the privileged. No hesitation in them. I wanted to be among them, too. The shop windows were a deep red and the cotton snow was real and old and glistened under the red of the lights. All of Ireland was in O'Connell Street. The buses moved slowly and the gray statues looked down on the crowds, making great gestures with their upraised arms that would free us all. All our messiahs. All gone, too. All in the books. Always late. Turned in. Disgraced. Exiled. They were another race, too. Held up before us. Made respectable by their agony. And still the crowds passed through O'Connell Street and nothing had changed at all. Sacrifices. Each day. One kind or another. They never smiled. No humor in them. Agony. Failure. Terrible failure. Wouldn't have it any other way. Like Jesus on the cross.

Still the half-crown burned in my pocket. I saw the huge bars of Cadbury's chocolate in their dark blue wrappers staring at me from the windows of the sweet shop. I stopped and stared back at them. The coin was on the tips of my fingers, and then I was walking through the door. I handed it over and took two bars in a white bag and walked out to the street. The gray was still hanging, and a mist was falling. I walked over the bridge and looked down into the dark waters. Desolate lonely, the dirty gulls flying close, scrounging and crying out over the roar of the buses. The tide was out and the smell rose up from the river. I felt the chocolate in my mouth. Christmas. All the Christmases that ever were, and I thought of my father standing before the ovens in the bakery. I wanted to have the white flour clinging to my arms and walk in his old, laceless boots with the tongues sticking out of them. I wanted to open the oven doors and feel the blast of heat in my face. To feel the sweat run down my back. To know the bread was done. To come home on the bus in the evening knowing I had done my day's work making the bread. I wanted to be like my father. What else was there to be?

"Don't be like me, son," he said.

Don't be like your father. No better man than your father.

In the middle of the week before Christmas it turned colder and it started to snow. They said it was a long time since it had snowed on Christmas week. It came down slowly as if it had known for a long time it would come that week. It sparkled in the light of the street lamps. I could see it through the bedroom window, and the room was brighter. When I looked out I could see all the way across to the nursery. The tall beech trees stood still, letting the snow caress them gently. All was silent. I knew it would be the loveliest Christmas we ever had. When I lay back in the bed, my throat throbbed with the beating of my heart; there was an elation so sweet that for an instant I couldn't swallow. In the snow-brightness of the bedroom I forgot all about the exam and the letter, and I knew there were only these days and they would last forever.

Paul was due any day, and when the snow showed no sign of stopping and kept coming down quietly my mother began to worry that he wouldn't be able to get home.

"Oh, he'll be here," my father said. "All too soon," but he smiled at her when he said it. "Sure it's only across the pond he has to come. Jesus he's not coming from China."

A day later the snow was still coming down and we had just finished tea in the evening. We were moving our chairs closer to the fire in the kitchen when there was a knock on the front door. I walked to the hallway and opened the door and there he was with the snow on his hair and the old suitcase resting on the doorstep. He was grinning at me. The wind whistled past the door and the snow was mad flying in all directions.

"Paul," I said, and I wanted to jump up and down.

"For Christ's sake take the suitcase, will ye. My hands are freezing. Jesus, there isn't a bus or a cab running from Dun-Laoghaire." I took the suitcase and burst into the kitchen.

"Paul is here," I said. My mother jumped up from the fire and ran into the hall, and Mary followed her. My father still sat in his chair and looked toward the door. I put the suitcase down, and then they were all in the kitchen and my mother was holding Paul and the snow fell from him onto her. Paul's head was buried in her shoulder and she wouldn't let him take it away. Mary had her arm around his waist and she leaned into him, smiling and looking at him. My father was standing with a half-smile on his face, waiting for them to stand apart. The front door was still open and the snow was billowing into the hall, whirling around. They finally stood back from each other and Paul saw my father standing before him and he reached out his hand. My father took it and smiled at him and Paul looked at him with his eyes raised. They moved back awkwardly from each other and my father sat down in his chair again.

"God, I'm freezing," Paul said as he moved to the fire. He held his hands close to it and then rubbed them together.

"Well, it's an odd time for you to be coming home, but it'll do," my mother said. "Now let me take a look at you." She looked him over. He was smiling at her, still rubbing his hands together as the melting snow ran down his face.

"Well, I don't know," she said to him. "I've seen you look better. You got thin. Jesus, there is hardly a pick on ye at all. You can't be eating. Not the way you look. My God, it must be awful over there."

"I'm all right," Paul said, aggravated. "Sure I eat enough."

"Well, good God, it doesn't look it," my mother said. "I don't like the look of you at all. I hope to God you won't go back to that bloody place. It never did anyone any good. They all look the same when they come back. I don't know what in the name of God it is." She put her arms around him again and held him to her. He was embarrassed. My father turned away and poked the fire and Mary put the kettle on for tea. Paul's eyes were full of surprise as my mother held him. He wanted to move away, but still I knew he was happy with her arms around him. His dark curly hair hung over his forehead, and my mother's eyes closed as she held him, breathing him in, and then finally she sighed and let him go.

"I have everything I want now," she said. "I have you here and we are all together for the Christmas. Wait till you see what we have. Wait till you see what we have."

"Oh, don't be talkin'," my father said. "Sure your poor mother has gone mad altogether. But sure we couldn't stop her. My God, there's enough in the house to feed the whole bloody British army. Aye, and the navy, too." The Christmas puddings were hanging, wrapped in cloth, over the fireplace, and there were huge cakes covered with almond icing sitting on the shelf near the window.

"Sure, my God, she has a turkey and a goose and a ham, too. You never seen the like of it," my father said. He was looking at my mother all the time he was talking. "I don't know where we are going to put it all."

"Oh, don't worry, mister," she said to him. "It won't go to waste. Sure, my God, the way they eat in this house you could never have enough."

Mary brought Paul a towel and placed it over his head, and she began to rub vigorously. "We don't want you to catch your death of cold," she said. When she stopped, his face was flushed and his hair was wild and he looked around and grinned at all of us.

"And we always wanted a white Christmas," Mary said, "but I think we're getting all the snow that never fell for all the other years."

"And England has it, too," Paul said. "I thought I'd never get out of London."

"And how was the crossing?" my mother asked him. "Sure we thought you mightn't get home at all."

"Well, you couldn't see your hand in front of your face," he told us. "It snowed all the way over. There weren't too many up on deck, and you couldn't get near the bar to get a drink." My mother looked at him for an instant without saying anything, and my father looked up from the fire and stared at his back. Paul's eyes were red with tiredness. He stretched his legs out before him and in an instant I saw him as I had always known him. His mad grin came to his face in a strange acknowledgment of something to himself. He was still with himself and his mad laughter. The mocking was still in him.

The fire roared up, and the kitchen glowed. The green walls hugged us all. We were in a distant place, far, far from the world. Where is London? There were only old times with us. Old joy. Old discoveries. Old warmth we always knew was there. The Christmas cards sat on the mantelpiece over the fire and all the Virgins looked out from them and the bald child with the halo and the outstretched arms floated over all the mangers. Sleds were pulled by reindeer and fat Santas smiled out at us, happy for our joy. Above the cards was the crucifix looking down, so far from the child.

"Well, anyway, thank God you're home," my mother said. "I was sure for a while there you wouldn't be able to come. I had my heart set on having you here. I don't know what I would have done if you hadn't come. But here you are. Now will you have a bite to eat? Sure, I hear the food there is terrible. Will you have a rasher? I know they are not to be had over there."

Paul nodded. "And it's still bad there," he said. "I'll tell you, though, it doesn't take much to please them. Oh, if they get a little extra once in a while they don't know themselves. They are not a bad crowd at all."

"Ah, the best in the world," my father said. "Oh, give me your English workingman any day. Nobody like them. And great for a bit of sport."

"Well, the chaps I work with are a grand crowd," Paul said. "Most of them back from the war."

"Well, what is it you do at all?" my father asked him. "In the odd letter that did come you never told us. Is it a factory or what?"

"Well, it's not really a factory. We put in boilers and do repairs and I work in the shop on parts and sometimes we go out on a job and they do central heating. Good money in it, too."

"Is it a trade?" my father asked him.

"Oh, it is," Paul said. "They have a union and everything."

"Well, you're working with your hands," my father said.

Paul nodded and looked at him with a trace of defiance in his face.

"Well, Jesus, you were never any good with your hands here," my father said to him. "You were like me. You couldn't hang a picture."

"And you still can't," my mother said to my father. "If there is anything to be done around here it's left to me."

"Well, now, Kelly," my father said, "why do you think I married you? I did have a bit of sense in me once. Aye, I did. I could have done a lot worse, but there you were with the hammer in your hand and, says I to meself, she's the one for me. Now if it hadn't been for the hammer sure I wouldn't have married you at all."

We laughed at him and he smiled, too, and winked at my mother. She tried to hide her own smile, as if she were annoyed, but he was flirting with her.

"And it was good of you to send the money to your mother," my father told him. "I'm glad you did that. That was manly." He winked and nodded at Paul.

Paul sat back in the chair and closed his eyes, his head resting on his chest. There was a half-smile on his face. He didn't look very different, but still I knew he was not the same as when he left. There was a sadness in him. Something was gone.

There was only Christmas Day itself left to wait for. My mother was relieved. She had waited, and now it had all come to her. She had managed through it all. All those years and now there was plenty and we were all together. She didn't worry about my father anymore. She had him back, and even if there was the odd time when he staggered home, sure, what of it? Wasn't he entitled to it now?

There was no word from the brewery. Nobody mentioned it anymore. There had been no exam. It didn't matter. There would be something else and if it didn't come now it would come right after Christmas. Sure, they wouldn't want me to start before Christmas anyway.

Paul had fallen asleep in the chair. I could see the dark stains from the nicotine on his fingers. They looked just like my father's, and now he slept in that same fierce way, his defiance and his pride in his sleeping face. Even as he slept, he questioned the world and all that was in it. His eyelids stared, as if he could see through them, and he held his head in a haughty questioning way. His lips were slightly pursed, as if he was already sure of what he would say when he awoke. There was something in him that I knew so well, something frightening and sad, a strange anger that always had him shaking his fist at the world. And then he would laugh at it and take his fist back. Why was I always so afraid for him?

His friends knocked on the door for him when they heard he was home. And in the evenings they went off together. I knew I would wait for him again as I used to before he went away. In those days before Christmas when the snow had fallen I felt that the world itself had come to a stop. Everything was covered with snow, there was a stillness and a peace. We saw everything by the light of the snow. We had put the world away. We didn't see the gray or the green or the blackness of the winter trees. The world itself was dressed up like the windows of the shops, and all the life went on in the silence pierced by the shouts of the children playing in the snow. They clustered around the snowy windows of the shops and stared into them, laughing, expecting more than they ever had before. It was all coming. The end and the beginning. Something was gone and something was coming. The sun shone down from the high blue sky and there was a brightness that had never been seen before. It was a smiling brightness, dazzling and fresh, and even in the snow there was all the warmth of the summer.

I lay in bed waiting for Paul to come home. I wanted him to talk to me. Surely he wouldn't be angry the way he used to be before. He could tell me about London. Had he gone to a big football match on a Saturday afternoon? Did he see Piccadilly Circus and Trafalgar Square? Did they know he was Irish? What are they like? Do you think I could go there, Paul? Oh, if we could put a net over this time. Could it always be that you have just come home? I heard the voices coming up the avenue and I felt the relief come over me. Soon he would be standing in the room. And then I heard the voices passing by the house, and I didn't hear them crying out their good nights. The gate didn't open and I didn't hear his steps on the path. He wasn't with them. The relief was gone and the anxiety came back. Where could he be? Why does he have to be out? Where could they have left him? What is there for him to do at this hour?

I sat up and stared out through the window. I could see the white snowy night. The world was frozen still. It stared back at me through the window. The night had him. He was always in the night. The benign night that came and stared and knew we were afraid. All the nights we had lain together.

I lay back down and wondered where he was. I slept again and dreamed that he was coming home from England and the boat went down in the Irish Sea. We were all on the top of Killiney Hill, looking out over the bay. The bay was lit up by the brightness of the snow, and we saw him sitting on the keel with his legs stretched out before him. There were soft snowflakes falling by the light of the moon and they sparkled in his hair and he smiled and waved to all of us. The boat began to slip under and still he smiled and waved.

The clock sounded three times and then the gate clanged and he was home. He came stumbling drunk up the stairs and he fell onto the bed and lay across me, his weight on me in the bed.

Christmas Day was my mother's day. Is there anything like the smell in the house on Christmas morning? The turkey in the oven and the gentle cooking sound. A soft crackling. The ham and the goose done the day before. The trifles sitting on the table. Food everywhere. Cakes and puddings. My mother's face beaming, all for the joy of having it. No shortage of anything. Abundance. We were not missing a thing. A Christmas like no other after all the years of deprivation. There wasn't room for another thing. And bottles of stout, too. And a bottle of whiskey. They had come up from Goggins's in the thick dark purple bags. And the breakfast that morning. The kitchen nearly floated away. The lovely red glow of the fire, and my father with black shoe polish shining his boots. I got new football boots that year, too. Beautiful soft black leather. I couldn't stop looking at them. I placed them in the middle of the kitchen floor and stood back and looked at them. Heavenly morning. Only room for joy. I couldn't take my eyes off them even as I sat at the table. I wanted to kiss them. Paul sat at the table smiling, looking out through his red eyes, his hair over his forehead, a cup of tea sitting before him. I never wanted to leave the house.

The kitchen was so bright. There were three new ties hanging around my father's neck, and my mother paused to wipe her hands on her apron while Mary made her try on her new gloves. She was embarrassed. New gloves. How long had it been since she had had a new pair? She held her hands out in front of her and beamed at them. She arched her arms and struck a pose like the ads in the newspaper and we laughed at her. And then Mary placed a lovely green scarf around my mother's neck. It was huge and it draped over her shoulders. She looked beautiful. Green was her color. Her hair was becoming whiter. She was like a queen who had found her palace again. My father looked at her and smiled. His eyes glistened and he sniffed and turned away. Always embarrassed at each other's joy. He had tenderness; he fought his tears. Paul looked on, too, opening and closing his eyes and batting his eyelids, all the time that mad smile on his face. Mary moved to my mother and gave her a hug, and then my mother turned away quickly and said, "You'll all be late for mass."

My father was ready. He wore one of his new ties and he kept fussing with the knot and stretching his neck and moving his chin back and forth. It looked perfect to me. Finally he turned around and faced us and said, "If you two hurry I'll walk down with you." I ran for my coat and Paul shaved quickly and when he was ready we all left together. The three of us walked together through the snow that was piled high. The sun was shining and the brightness dazzled us. The sky was a deep blue, nearly purple, dancing before our eyes. I walked between my father and Paul. I felt safe and new. I had never been with them in that way and now we nodded and saluted everyone who passed us and my father kept saying, "God that's a morning." And he said, "I've never seen your mother so happy. Did you see her with the gloves on? Oh, she's in heaven. Sure my God I've never seen her look forward to anything the way she did to this day." Paul nodded and stared ahead. The wind was blowing softly, and we walked into it. I wanted to pull them with me and run and jump and laugh out loud.

It seemed that everyone we passed wore something new. There were only smiles that morning. I wore the blue coat my aunt had sent me from America. They all looked at it and it was soft and blue the same color as the sky. The church looked new that morning, too. It was covered with snow. The granite sparkled in the sun, warm and sure and solid. The inside was like a wonderful warm cave decorated with ivy and holly. The ivy hung from the window ledges, and the church was green and red. The white marble of the altar looked delicate and fragile, ready for the sacrifice. Ready for the death. Standing between heaven and earth. But the church was full of life that morning and there was nodding and greeting and smiles. It could float away and take us all with it up through the blue skies.

I glanced up at the balcony, and Johnny Seery was there, staring down as if he were making strange judgments of us. He had no new clothes. He wore the same old coat and the ancient tie and the old white shirt that was gray with age. He would be walking the roads forever, seeing everything. Pumping the organ. What did he get for Christmas?

I knelt between Paul and my father. They stared ahead at the altar and I could see how much they looked alike. Their lips were slightly pursed in an attitude of prayer. As the priest made his way through the mass, they stood and sat, making the responses in voices I could hardly hear. There was no fervor in them, nor resignation, only habit.

The priest moved on the altar by habit, too, and at the sermon he said all the things I had heard him say so many times before. I wanted the mass to be over so that I could visit the crib. When Aunt Lill wrote to us each year at Christmas she always said the same thing. "I will remember you all in my poor prayers as I visit the infant Jesus in the manger on Christmas morning." And when the priest left the altar, I went to the crib and kneeled before it. It was done like a cave of dark gray stone, the shepherds and the animals and Mary and Joseph around the manger. The Child lay back with his head raised, his arms outstretched as though He wanted to embrace us all. I saw the looks on the faces of Mary and Joseph and the gentle shepherds holding the lambs. There were cows in the back breathing on the Child, keeping Him warm, and there was a star in the sky over the entrance to the cave, giving out its light. There was a light that came from the Child, his innocent face looking so expectantly at us. He was plump and big for his age; the center of attention, looking at us with a trace of amazement on his face. He seemed to think that we should all know Him already. How could we have gone on for so long without knowing?

Paul and my father stood behind me, staring in at the figures. The same crib every year. The deep cave dark at the back and once in a while a small light appeared out of nowhere. Was it real or did I think I saw it?

The table was set in the living room when we came home. It was covered with the beautiful pink linen tablecloth, and the turkey and the goose and the ham made a column down its center. Everything was in its place. The decorations hung in arches from the ceiling, and a huge green colored bell hung from the center. There was holly over all the pictures, and the sideboard held the trifles and the puddings, the cakes. There was a huge clear glass bowl full of custard and another with jelly that was a deep maroon. There were open boxes of chocolates tempting us all and the fire was lit. The afternoon sun shone in on us through the white curtains so bright that we could hardly see the flames of the fire. In a corner on the floor stood the bottles of stout in their gray bags, and in their company was the lovely amber bottle of Jameson's.

My grandfather arrived with Aunt Elizabeth, my mother's sister, and Uncle Jim, her brother. All the extra chairs were brought to the table and they called out the greetings. "Happy Christmas. Happy Christmas." My mother stood and admired her sister's new coat. My grandfather kept lighting up his new pipe and letting it go out.

"But God, did you ever see a Christmas like it?" he said. "It's only perfect. All the snow before it and now the day itself and it's like summer. Sure, Jesus, Johnny, we must be coming to the end of the world."

"Ah, never mind," my father said. "We'll take it, end of the world or no." He walked to the corner and brought the stout to the table.

"And is that yourself, Paul?" my grandfather said. "Sure God I hardly know you anymore. You're the spit of your father. And they didn't kill you over there."

Paul smiled at him, and Uncle Jim and my father opened the bottles of stout, leaving them stand, and then they passed the glasses. Paul got up and brought a bottle of stout to the table for himself and poured it into the glass, tilting it, letting the head build.

"God, you do that well," my grandfather said, winking at him.

"Ah, sure, to some of us it comes natural," Paul said, and then my grandfather raised his glass and said, "Well here's a happy Christmas," and lifted the glass to his lips. His mouth shivered as he drank, then he carefully placed the glass back down on the table, the tan foam clinging to his mustache. He closed his eyes for an instant, overcome with the taste, and then he opened them and squinted and smiled.

"Jasus, that's a good pint," he said.

The others nodded as they drank and my mother said, "Come on now before everything gets cold." The plates were passed around so full they couldn't take any more. My mother saw to it that everything was brimming over and when there was a plate before everyone she finally sat down herself.

"Well, God has been good to us," she said. We all nodded. "It was a long time coming," she said. "But it was all worth waiting for. I'll never forget the year we had the little cake and hardly a mouthful for everyone."

"O Cathleen, them was tough times all right," my grandfather said. "Tough times."

"God, it was as if Ireland was the last place in the world," my mother said. "All that was going on in the world, and we with not enough to make a cake with."

"Ah, the world is a bloody strange place all the same," my grandfather said. "Sure God, how long is it since we had a turkey and a goose and a ham?"

"Oh, nothing would do her but to have them all," my father said. "There was no stopping her."

"Sure it was only for the once I wanted to see us not needing anything. Look at all the years I've been saying go easy on the butter, and sometimes not a drop of milk in the house, or the times when I had nothing to give Johnny for his lunch. Aye, and there were times he went off in the morning with little or nothing. And sure you know Johnny. As long as he had the price of a few cigarettes he was all right."

She looked around the table at us all. "There are still plenty of poor souls with not a thing on the table today. Aye, for them there is no difference, Christmas or any other day."

"Well, rich or poor, there is few have a table before them the like of this," my grandfather said.

"That's the truth, Cathleen," Aunt Elizabeth said. "I don't know how you managed to get everything. I've never seen the like of it."

"Oh, God, Cathleen, the turkey is delicious," said Uncle Jim. "Oh, Johnny, sink your teeth into that. Did you get that in Dempsey's? Oh, that's a bird and a half for you. He gave you a good one all right. How long is it since we had a turkey? God, it must have been before the war. I don't know what in the name of God happened to the turkeys when the war started. Strange where they all went."

"Every bloody thing went to the war," my grandfather said. "Jesus, there were times we were lucky to get a box of matches. But we came through it all. It left us none the worse." He chewed his food with great satisfaction and looked around the table. There was an instant when all the mouths were full and they all concentrated and savored, taking the feast before them. They were making up for all the years.

"And isn't it grand that Paul came home," Aunt Elizabeth said. "Well now, you couldn't have come at a better time. And you came to the right house, too."

"True enough," my father said. "Times is still hard over there. I don't know that it will ever be right again for them. But God, they do have the way of going through it. I suppose you have to hand it to them."

"Ah, well now, Johnny, they go in for that sort of thing," my grandfather said. "They love to have their backs up. Grand the way they all pull together. Great spirit they have. Sure they don't know what to do with themselves when the times is good." He looked around at us with his eyebrows raised and a smile on his face. His fork was poised, holding a piece of turkey.

"But all the same now, you have to hand it to them. They are a marvelous people," my father said.

"Ah, hand them me arse," said Uncle Jim. He didn't look up from his plate. "Didn't they hand us ours for long enough." They all looked at him. His head was buried in his plate and he chewed furiously.

"Well Jesus, Jim, I can see that you haven't changed," my father said.

"Ah, don't pay any attention to him," my grandfather said. "All that bloody crowd that drinks up in Dowd's is the same. Pissin' and moanin', wearin' their medals. Bloody crowd of chancers."

"And does auld Hanlon still go in there?" my father asked.

"Oh, indeed and he does," my grandfather said. "Sure that fella has a medal for everything. Oh, he'd have you believe he stood next to Patrick Pearse in the post office. Some of them would say anything to get a job. They were all there when the jobs were handed out. And most of them still in nappies when the troubles were on. But I suppose you can't blame them. Sure Jesus isn't there hundreds for every job that opens up?"

"It's bloody funny all the same to see them marching in the parades and the bloody half of them wasn't born when it was on. And them all wearing medals."

"Oh, the medals are easily had, Johnny," my grandfather said. "Sure, Jasus, you can get them in any pub. Any kind you want. And if medals could get them jobs they'd all be working."

He looked at Paul and said, "I suppose there's plenty of work in England."

"Oh, plenty," Paul said, looking up from his plate. "Not enough for the jobs. Still an awful lot of men in the services."

"Well, isn't it a strange bloody thing all the same," my grandfather said, "they have all the jobs and no grub and we with all the grub and no jobs? Bloody strange world altogether. Sure if it's not one thing it's another. And I hear London is still in a terrible state."

"Oh, it is," Paul said. "Nearly everywhere you go you see the bombed-out buildings. It will take a long time to put it right. But still there is a lot of life in it. You have to hand it to them."

"Ah, but there is no place like our own," Uncle Jim said. "I heard that said by many a chap that's been away. Fellas that have been all over the world. Always glad to come back."

"Oh, true enough," my father said. "I've always heard that.

And sure the furthest meself and Cathleen ever got was Liverpool when we were married. I'll never forget sitting in a park there and the soot falling down out of the sky, landing on the arm of my new suit. True as God. Bloody big lump of soot landed on me. A grand place all the same. They say there's more Irish there than in Dublin. Oh, you'd have to take a long ramble before you'd find a place like Dalkey or Killiney. Sure God, some mornings when I'd take a walk on the Vico Road and see out over the bay and the sun coming up. Oh, don't be talkin'. Sure, don't they say it's as beautiful as the Bay of Naples. It must be lovely up there now with the snow. It's a rare time you'd see Killiney Hill covered with snow. I've seen it, though. I've looked down the bay toward Bray Head and it covered with snow. There was a sight for you. And you'd see the fields covered reaching back from the head. And the red sky of an early morning over the bay. God's truth you couldn't tell if it was morning or evening. It didn't matter good or bad times. You couldn't tell." They all nodded and then they were silent.

"There's plenty more, now," my mother said. "Father, come on now. Give me your plate. And Paul, are you ready for more?" They held their plates up and she filled them again and looked out over us quick to see where she could add more to our plates, determined to make us eat as much as possible.

"It's terrible all the same that so many have to go away. Many's the poor mothers and fathers has to watch them leave."

"Well, it's a terrible bloody country can't provide for its own," Paul said.

"What are you talking about?" my father said, staring. "Weren't you well provided for? Sure Jasus, many's the fella would have jumped at the chance you had. You had your chance."

"Chance for what?" Paul shot back at him. "Chance for what? To be a bloody laborer in the brewery for the rest of my life. All taken care of. Bloody clerks calling you by your last name."

"Ah, what of it?" my father said. "What the bloody hell do you care what they call you by. Sure Jesus, wasn't it the best bloody job in Dublin? Let them call you what they want. Jesus, you were easily put off. If that's all it takes."

Paul looked at him and the mad smile appeared on his face, and then he looked back down into his plate. My father still looked at him as if he were waiting for him to say something.

"Ah, wait till you see," said Uncle Jim. "There will be all sorts of changes now that things are getting back. All sorts of schemes. Factories. Sure they'll be putting up factories and building houses. Sure Jesus they'll have to."

"You can't even get a decent education in this bloody country," Paul said. "At least in England you don't have to pay."

"And what would a bloody education do for them?" my father said. "Education won't change a bloody thing. Not there nor here, either. Just makes them want more. Gives them the idea they know better than them that went before them. Bloody education. Wasted on the half of them. Jesus, education and the arses out of their trousers." Paul looked out from under his eyelashes and then turned back to his plate. My mother looked at him and caught his eye, shaking her head, asking him to understand.

"And wait till you see what happens with the factories," my father said. "They'll all go bloody mad. Oh, you'll see changes all right. They'll all be looking for more bloody money. Sure they go mad now with a few bloody shillings in their pockets. Sure, don't the most of us only want to make a living and not have to sweat too hard for it. What the hell is there besides that? A man to be with his own family and not have to break his back. Bloody factories. What is it we want to do? Bring England here?"

They fell silent again. My mother looked at Aunt Elizabeth and closed her eyes, hoping the moment would pass.

"And what about Jackie?" my grandfather asked. "No word from the brewery yet?" I looked at him and shook my head.

"Ah, don't worry, now," my mother said. "He'll get it."

"Sure, don't I know he will," my grandfather said, looking toward me. "Don't worry, auld son. We'll all be dead a long time. Aye indeed. Eat your dinner."

My mother was looking at Paul "You've hardly touched a thing," she said to him. "That's a terrible pity. You won't see the likes of this when you go back. You should eat it now while you can. Are you not yourself? God, I've seen you with more color in you."

"I'm all right," he said. "I'm just tired. I got very tired coming home. It was a long time to be traveling."

"Aye," my mother said, shaking her head. "And you've been up till all hours of the morning. You haven't even taken any kind of a rest. Gallivanting since you came home."

Paul closed his eyes and leaned back from the table. He reached behind him and put a bottle of stout on the table, and then he began to pour it. He sat back in the chair, looking at the glass, and the old merriment was in his eyes. My mother was looking at the glass in front of him, then she turned away as though she didn't want to see it. There was a look he had that always vexed her. He had taken himself away. He didn't join them in their talk now. He didn't argue. "You're too full of argument," my mother used to say to him, and now he hadn't said much at all.

My mother began to reach out for the empty plates. We

passed them up to her, and she and Mary brought them out to the kitchen. They came with the dessert plates and placed them before us, and when they came to Paul he looked up and said, "No, not for me."

"Oh, come now, Paul," Mary said. "Will you not have a piece of pudding with the custard over it? It's the good custard. It will give you all the luck for the New Year."

He looked at her and shook his head, a wan smile on his face.

"Well, don't get into too much of that," my father said, pointing to his glass.

He raised his eyes and looked at my father. He was looking out past us all. I wondered what he could see.

Mary and my mother served the pudding with the lovely yellow custard over it. "Oh, God, Cathleen, that's the best you ever made," my grandfather said. We all looked up and nodded and my mother smiled and tasted her own and smiled. "O Paul, won't you?" Mary asked him again, but he only raised his eyes and barely shook his head.

They sat back from the table when they had finished, and the blue smoke from their cigarettes drifted up to the ceiling. The sun still shone brightly, and if it weren't for the snow I would have believed it was summer. The women began to clear the table and the cats sat on the windowsill in the sun, staring in at us. My grandfather sat back with his hands clasped over his stomach and his pipe in his mouth. His eyes were closed and there was a silver cover over his pipe. He puffed occasionally, even though it wasn't lit. Paul stared at his glass as though he couldn't see it.

We could hear the shouts of the children on the avenue. The new toys were brought out into the snow. I wanted to wear my football boots and run in the field with them and feel them on my feet. How I had looked at them that morning and held them up high over my head so that I could see them from every angle. I couldn't wait to put them on.

"Are you going up to the field?" Paul asked me.

"I think I will," I said. "I want to try my boots."

"I'll take a walk up there with you," he said.

"Aye, that would be good for you," my mother said, nodding her head. "Did you ever see such a day? Sure it's like the summer. It'll do you good to be out in it. Off with you both now."

"I'm going to wear the boots," I told them. "Maybe some of the lads will be up there and we can have a game."

We left the house and walked through the snow toward the field. The sky was still the lovely blue as if it had never seen a cloud. The snow glistened, and we were dazzled by the brightness. The avenue was full of children pulling toys, leaving tracks in the snow. They had thrown their jackets off and they ran shouting, playing games, joining hands and moving in circles, sliding and diving in the snow as if it were the sea in summer. The doors to all the houses were open; the mothers and fathers looked out smiling, surprised and amazed at the day. They spoke across the garden hedges to each other, nodding.

"Did you ever see such a day?" they said. "Did you ever see such a day?"

Paul hardly spoke as we walked. Even with the sun shining down its gentle warmth, his collar was turned up and his head was pulled down into his chest. He didn't look around. He didn't see the great carnival all around him. Even when they called his name from the houses as we passed, he barely looked and only made a slight movement with his head. He wouldn't stop. He walked quickly toward the field, in a hurry to leave them behind. We reached the field and ducked through the small opening in the hedge.

There were some boys kicking a football, but it would not move over the snow. It became stuck every time it landed. Still they played and kicked it again as the snow clung to their legs. The goalposts stood gaping, looking out with the marks of hundreds of games on them, dark against the snow. They always stood, never moving, staring, looking out over the field impassive even when the ball sped through them for a goal.

Paul used to play goalie, but now he didn't even look toward the players. His head was bowed as we walked up through the field in the white. I wanted him to talk to me, but he didn't speak. I turned my head toward him and stared. He felt me looking at him. He turned his eyes to me and barely smiled; then he turned away again. His hands were in his pockets, and he walked fast. I could see our two shadows in the snow. His eyes were like an idiot's, with a life of their own.

When we reached the low wall near the woods, he sat down and took a small bottle from his pocket and drank a long swallow. The melting snow ran down the trees behind us and they sparkled and glistened in the sun. We could hear the shouts of the players, and we saw them race across the snow in their colored jerseys. We could hear the clang of the churns from the dairy at the top of the field. Paul was so far away from me, sitting on the wall, and I watched him with the bottle held to his lips, his head tilted back. He brought it forward again, holding the liquid in his mouth. He swallowed and stared across the field. I wanted to go and join in the game, but I couldn't leave him. I wanted to talk to him. I wanted to say the thing that would bring him back, but I didn't know what it was. A cry went up as a goal was scored. The voices of those scored against were cursing at each other, blaming and scornful, while the others were joyful, hugging one another. Paul only stared past them to a distant place, drinking from the bottle.

Some of the players saw me and waved me over to the game, but I shook my head and sat by Paul, wondering what was wrong with him. After a while he swung his legs over the wall and started into the woods, and I followed behind him. I wondered where he would go. We ducked under the branches, knocking the snow from them. It fell down on us, disturbed and wet, clinging. He kept turning around, looking at me, the mad smile on his face, his eyes wild. There was a knowing, a resolve in him. He hummed softly to himself as we made our way through the trees. He quickened his walk, and my face was wet from the snow. I had to run to keep up with him. He was running through the trees laughing his mad laugh, and he flung the empty bottle high up into the branches. It came crashing back down, knocking the snow from the trees, and then it splintered and the pieces lay around the bottom of a tree. He still ran and looked back, waving to me to follow him as he shouted and laughed. Then we came to a clearing and he stopped. He began to unbutton his fly, and he pissed toward the sky, rising up on his toes.

"Come on, do your piss. Do your piss. See how far it can go. Oh, look at that. Look at that. That's Guinness's for you. Piss it out again. Come on now, for Jasus sake do your piss."

The great stream ran from him, landing on the snow, leaving its scribbled patterns. Then I began to piss, too. I was frightened but I couldn't help laughing at him. Then when he was finished he stood looking at me.

"Come on, for Jasus sake," he said. "You can go higher than that."

I strained and lifted myself onto my toes and put all my strength into the flow as I watched it speed out, making an arc. Then it fell back down into the snow.

"Not bad," he said. "Not bad," and then he began to walk again.

I followed behind him. Then without turning his head he said, "Do you think I'm mad, Jackie?"

"No," I said to his back, and he turned around smiling.

"Wait till I tell you what I have seen. Do you want to know it all? O Jackie, they're not nearly as smart as us. With all their learning. They don't have nearly as much. All the same, they only listen to you if you have the learning. I could run rings around most of them. I suppose they're all right, the English, but still a strange bloody crowd. All love their mothers. The husbands don't call their wives by their first names. 'Mother! Mother,' they say. You should hear them." He laughed out loud, sharing the story with himself.

"All the husbands are quiet. Not a word out of them. Never raise their voices. Not like our own auld fella. Never hear a word from them." He was drunk now, and he stared off in a reverie, as if he had discovered a great joke.

"You don't have to go back there, Paul. You could stay. What do you have to go back for?"

"I can't stay, Jackie. I just can't stay. O Jackie, all the things I wanted to do. I don't know where I want to go but I can't stay here. But I saw Arsenal play."

"Did you?"

"Sixty thousand at the game. They played Tottenham. Terrific."

"Sixty thousand!"

"It was a draw."

The path through the woods was still too narrow for the two of us, and I wanted to move up to him and see his face. I was at his side for an instant, and I saw the fright on him, as if he didn't know where to turn or what to do. We turned off the path at the place where the hut was. He stopped at a holly bush that was covered with snow. The red berries shyly looked out in their tiny clusters. He broke some stems from the bush, and we walked on again until we came to the hut. He turned and looked at me, smiling, and he said, "It's still here," and he crawled in through the opening as I followed him. "I wonder if there is still a candle here," he said. I could hear him moving around. "The nights we had here with Davin and Roe. I suppose they never come up here now. Surprised the old hut is still standing."

He still moved around, then he lit a match, moving it along the walls, looking for a place. "I found one," he said while he held the small butt of a candle before him, lighting it. He grinned at me, and his hair was hanging over his forehead, his eyes shining. "No place like home," he said, pulling another small bottle from his pocket. He sat down against the wall and held the bottle to his lips and swallowed, and then he let out a long sigh.

"Ah, yes," he said. "Ah, yes." He was breathing deeply as if he had just run a race or played in a great game. He placed the bottle on the ground beside him, then he took the holly stems, joining them together, and placed them on his head.

"Julius Caesar," he said, laughing, and shook his head. "Jesus Christ with me berries and me green leaves. I know one man couldn't put this on his head. Gandhi. Couldn't put holly on his baldy head." I laughed at him and he leaned his head back against the wall. He drank from the bottle and closed his eyes.

"Do you think I'm mad?" he asked me again. "If I'm not, I know I will be. But sure aren't I mad already? They don't know what to do with me. The way they look at me. He's a terror, they say. Is there a place for him? They'd rather have me respectable and die for them in Guinness's. Wearing the little messenger's hat, running around. I'd rather be like

Johnny Seery and walk the roads. I don't want to do anything. I don't want to do anything at all. Like the tramps who come around every year and knock on the door asking for a bit of sugar or a pinch of tea. Happy as Larry. Or I could go with the tinkers and mend the pots and pans. Do you think I could do that? Ah sure I don't know what I'm talking about. I don't know what the notions are that are in my head. Jasus, even the things I used to think I wanted. Let them have them. None of us belong to it the way it is. I don't even know how to say it. Even the auld fella. They don't have an idea. Some kind of loyalty they have to something. . . . Ah sure Jasus I don't know what I'm saying and you don't know what I'm talking about."

He drank from the bottle. I could see the amber-colored liquid moving in the light of the candle. His head hung down, and he began to talk in a low whisper.

"I get such a bloody ache. Such an ache that I don't know where it comes from. Sure I've always had it, I think. It turns over in me. I don't know, Jackie. Is it that I'm mad? Maybe I'm as mad as any of them in there with Audrey. I could sit in the hut here and never move for the rest of my life."

The hut was covered in the soft light of the candle. I could see the wet running down the stone wall. His eyes were red and tired and they were full of a terrible fright. I wanted to cry and hold onto him, but I knew he would be angry if I did. He would turn on me; his angry voice would be just like my father's. The anger that was always a defeat. Always out of some deep hurt that was unfathomable. Always as if some ancient place was pierced. It came, and then the doors closed again as if they were afraid to look at where it came from. We could never face it, and we all trembled before it, and somehow we all knew we had to let it pass by.

If we stayed too long before it, we would surely all go mad. We pretended all was well. It was economics and the war and the way the world was. Everything was going to be better. All over like a wedding. Wait till you see. Now that didn't hurt at all, did it? Enough for a drink and a smoke and all was well. All the hearts showed themselves vaguely to each other, and they sensed the pain, and they all walked around it, denying it.

I was frightened. Some terrible thing had happened to Paul that I couldn't reach. I stared down at my football boots, and they were like two strangers to me. I didn't care that I had them on. I looked at Paul, wanting to shake him. To plead with him. Slipping away the way he did. Always going away from me. I raised my head to him, ready to plead and beg to reach across the madness. I could feel all the rage rising up in me, and I wanted to kick at him and to spit. I wanted to fling all my violence toward him in a terrible shock, to release him from the deep place that held him. It all formed a terrible shout. It was formless, a cry, then I kicked at him. He leaped up and flung me against the wall.

"You little twerp. You fuckin' little twerp," he snarled at me through his clenched teeth. I ran toward him again and he flung me back. My head hit the soft muddy wall and I was stunned. It rang as I lay on the ground. He stood over me breathing heavily, looking down with the madness in his eyes. I wanted to spit at him. What was it that would satisfy him?

"Be Paul! Be Paul, you're not Paul. What do you want? What do you want?"

He stared down at me, and for an instant the strangeness left his eyes. He was going to say something, but then he flung the bottle against the wall and turned and crawled out through the entrance.

The black clay of the ceiling looked down at me, and I wondered where I was. He was gone and I couldn't move. I felt the tears run down my face, and all the fright was in my chest. A terrible fright. My head was aching, and I wanted to reach out and hold him and tell him to come back. I moved toward the opening and came out into the air. I stood looking toward the path, but he was gone.

"Paul. . . . Paul. . . ." I cried after him. The trees stood still and the frightened birds lifted from them. They made their sounds and passed up into the sky. The snow lay still and peaceful, covering everything. I could see his footprints leading to the path, and I held my head in my hands and shivered. Maybe he'll be home when I get there. It's always something with him. Always some bloody thing. Nothing is ever right for him. He'd pick an argument with God Himself. My mother even said that. "Jasus, you're never happy," she'd say to him. "I don't know what in the name of God it takes with you. You'd break my heart. I don't know what it is you want."

When I reached the field the game was over. I could see the fellows straggling down the field toward the avenue. I stood back because I didn't want to walk with them. I could see the roofs of the houses and the smoke from the fires slowly moving up to the sky. The evening was coming down, and the sky was turning red. There were no mad clouds chasing across as they often did. There was only the red. I moved to the wall where we had sat before and swung my legs over it. I sat and kicked my heels against the wall. I didn't want to go home. I didn't want the night to start. The Banshee time.

The visitors were gone when I got home. My mother and father and Mary were sitting around the fire in the kitchen.

"Where's Paul?" Mary asked me when I walked in.

"He went off," I told them.

"Jesus, you'd think he'd come home this one night," my father said, looking at my mother.

"Oh, I suppose he went off with the fellas," she said. She looked tired and pleased with the day. She sat before the fire with her knitting, still wearing her apron. Her feet were out of her slippers, and she leaned back in her chair, happy.

"That fella always finds a way to aggravate," my father said. "He sat through the dinner grinning at us like we were all some sort of bloody fools. Jesus, there were times there I could have killed him. If it wasn't for your father and the others I would have flattened him. God's truth. And him looking at us all with the pint before him, showing us. He could just as well have shook his fist at us. He's a cur."

"Ah, Johnny, he was only tired," my mother said to him with a soft smile on her face. "Sure, he only sat there."

"Don't I know," my father said with his eyes raised and his head thrust back. "He just sat there like Lord Muck looking at all the bloody fools around him. I tell you that fella has a way of provoking. I'm damn sure if he keeps it up he won't last very long. No place would put up with it. He's still a mocker and a jeerer. Jesus, he grates on me." He turned back to the fire, his eyes staring fiercely, and then he turned to me and said, "Where did he go?"

"I don't know," I said quietly.

He turned away from me and looked back into the fire and he said, "I suppose he went up to Silk's to pour some more drink into himself. Christmas night and your mother after slaving after him all day. Bloody chancer." He turned back to the fire.

"Ah, Johnny, don't ruin the day for yourself, now," my mother pleaded. "Sure, won't he be going back soon enough?"

"Jesus, it won't be soon enough for me," my father said.

Mary looked at me with her eyes raised in a question. There was anguish in her look, and she shared it with me as though she knew there was something wrong. She looked away and held her hands together in her lap, staring at them. We listened to the carols on the radio, and then the wind began to come up. It raced around the house and rattled the windows, then the huge drops of rain came hurtling down with a great anger. The wind came roaring down the chimney and pushed the smoke out at us.

"Jesus, that was sudden," my father said, looking toward the window.

"And the skies were red when I was walking home," I told him.

"Ah sure, you'd never know, son," my father said. "In this bloody country you never know what happens till it's here."

The rain pelted down and the wind grew stronger. The doors rattled and the trees moaned. We could hear the sound of things being blown over and the slamming of doors and shouts.

"God, there'll be flooding if that keeps up," my father said.

"And Paul out in it," my mother said.

"Oh, trust him," said my father. "I never saw anything like him. The way he can put his foot in it."

My mother looked at him, disappointed. She didn't like to hear what he said, and I could see the worry begin to come over her.

"Well, I'm sure there's many was caught out in it," she told him. "I'm sure he's not the only one." A great puff of dark smoke came whirling down the chimney, and the wind whistled in an agony. I could hear the rain pouring down the gutters, flinging itself to the ground in a mad tumult. The gusts slammed into the house, hitting it like bombs. At times it seemed they would pick it up and take us all away.

"I hope to God he's out of it someplace," my mother said. "I hope to God he's not stuck somewhere."

"Oh, don't worry about that fella," my father said. "Sure he's probably with Sweeney or McAuley. The way that crowd talks, sure they wouldn't notice an earthquake. Oh, they're all up there on their soapboxes yammering away, and none of them listening to the other. All talking at the one time and not an ounce of sense in any of them. Anyway, Kelly, you've had a long day. Don't be worrying about your man."

She nodded, and the old look of worry was on her face. She put her knitting down on the chair beside her and then she stood up. She moved over to the window and pressed her eyes to the glass.

"God, I can't see a thing," she said. "It's a terrible night. You'd think he'd have come home."

"For God's sake, don't start now," my father said. "You never know with that fella. Let him be. Don't worry. He'll ramble in here, not able to stand up, and he'll laugh at all of us and fall into his bed. Come on now, Kelly. Up with you." She turned away from the window and nodded.

"Well it's been a lovely Christmas," she said.

"And you still have enough in the house to feed the bloody army," he said, smiling at her. "Sure Jasus, Kelly, by the looks of it you won't have to do any shopping next Christmas."

She looked at Mary and me and she smiled. "Well, I'll leave you," she said. "Good night. Don't stay up too late yourselves." We looked at her, and then she turned away.

"Good night," we said together, and my father walked behind her. I heard them on the stairs; then the bedroom door closed.

Mary and I sat in the kitchen. She moved to my mother's chair and sat with her feet on the fender. The wind battered the house, buffeting it, time after time. I looked at Mary, but I could not bring myself to tell her what had happened.

"Where could he be?" she said at last. "My God, on a night like this. Where in the name of God could he be? He must be mad to be out in this." I couldn't answer her, and I stared into the fire.

"He's not himself since he's been home," she said. "I don't know what it is. I don't know why I worry about him the way I do. But Jackie, I've always worried about him. He's not like you. I don't know what it is that's in him. He'd break your heart. He's always been that way, but still they always came knocking at the door for him. Even before he went away, Jackie, he left them behind. They stopped coming the way they used to. He started going off on his own. Nobody ever knows where he goes. Nobody sees him. Coming home at three and four in the morning. Where in the name of God does he go?"

Raindrops came down the chimney, hissing onto the fire, and the light kept moving slightly. There was a knock on the front door, and I leaped up to see who was there but when I opened the door there was no one and I realized it was only the wind. I stared out into the night and I could see the rain falling by the streetlights, its direction changing at every mad gust of wind. Mary came into the hallway. She looked out, too, trying to see something, and then we both turned away and went back to the fire. Even as we sat, the knocker sounded again. We could hear the tiles being blown from the roof, then hitting the road with a faint tinkling that was gone as soon as it was heard.

My father's snoring stopped. I heard him in the bedroom and then there was the sound as he used the chamber pot. It always seemed to go on forever, on and on until I thought the pot would overflow. Then we heard him at the top of the stairs and he called down to us.

"Don't stay up much longer now. God knows what time your man will be home." We heard the bedroom door close and Mary looked at me.

"I think I'll go up," she said to me, and she looked as if she would cry. "Don't stay up too long yourself. You can't wait for him. He'll be home when he comes home." Her brown eyes were soft, and then she turned and I heard her going up the stairs.

My football boots stood by the fire with the mud caked on them from the field. They would never be the same again. I went to the larder and opened it and the turkey lay ravaged but still with plenty of meat on it. There was a lovely dark drumstick and I wanted to bite into it but I knew it was for my father. I started to pick from the plate and soon my mouth was full and for the time I forgot about Paul. The first turkey and the taste of it clinging to my mouth. I wanted to pull it apart. The stuffing still lay deep in its belly, and I reached in with my hand and pulled it out and ate it from my fingers, and then I took a wing and brought it back to the fire with me. I chewed it until there was nothing left on it, and then I threw it into the fire.

I moved to my father's chair and sat in the same way that he did, with my feet resting on the fender. I could feel the warmth of the fire on my feet, and I fell asleep.

I awoke to the sound of the knocker, and all over the house there was another sound as if it were being beaten with sticks. It was on the roof and in the walls and the wind had raised its voice beyond a howl to a terrible sharp piercing shriek. I could feel the force of it against the house, the terrible fury of it. The house clung to the ground, afraid for itself. I looked around and saw all the things in the kitchen, the pots and pans, the crockery in the dresser and the pictures on the walls and they too were clinging to their places, afraid they would be ripped away. The light went out, and I jumped up from the chair and ran to the switch and moved it back and forth, but still it wouldn't go on. I went to the living room and looked out the window. It was pitch black. There was nothing to be seen. The streetlights had long since gone out. There was only blackness rolling over everything, covering all in its heavy waves and the voices of the storm going on inside it. No sign of Paul. I knew it wasn't like the other nights. It was beyond all the anxiety of the other times. He would always be gone. Always away from us. He wouldn't stay. Couldn't wait to get away.

I went back to the kitchen in the dark, and I could see the red glow from the fire. There wasn't much of it left. The wind pestered the white ashes and pulled them up and out into the night. I sat in the chair and I began to cry softly to myself. All the knocking and banging went on as if the night were full of madmen and the dead had joined them. All the dead marching down Sutton's Hill banging on the doors and the roofs and the walls of the houses. Could he be in the hut? I'll go up to the hut and see if he's there. I leaned toward the fire and pulled the football boots toward me. I began to put them on and the kitchen door opened and my father stood there.

"My God, are you still up?" he asked me. I looked at him.

"The lights are all out," I said. "Oh, I'm sure the wires are down all over the place."

"Where are you going with those boots on?" he asked me. I didn't answer him.

"Come on, now, mister," he said. "Up to bed with you. God knows when the other fella will be home. Up you go now." I walked past him to the stairs and he followed up behind me. "Go to sleep now."

I lay down on the bed with my clothes on and then I fell asleep.

He hadn't come home when I awoke in the morning. The wind still blew, but the rain had stopped. I heard the voices in the kitchen, and I could smell the bacon. I looked out the window toward the nursery. The snow was almost gone. I could see the dark plowed field again with remnants of the white. The dark trees stood silently. I had thought the snow would stay forever, but it was gone. I knew there would be a night when he wouldn't come home. I could not allow myself to wonder why he hadn't come. The gray clouds sped across the sky, and the sun was weak and afraid, not ready yet to stay.

I went down to the kitchen, and they looked at me when I walked in, but nobody said anything. I sat at the table, and my mother put a cup of tea before me. My father was reading the paper and smoking. He sat staring into the paper, his shirtsleeves rolled up. My mother looked at me, her lovely soft green eyes full of fear.

"That was a terrible storm," my father said finally. "They say the waves were coming up over the seafront road last night. The mail boat didn't come in, either. There wasn't any crossings. They say the harbor is in a terrible state."

"And all that after the lovely day it was yesterday," my mother said. "God, it came fast, and it wasn't forecast at all. It was like a summer's day, and not a breath of wind. I never heard anything like that wind last night. I thought the house would be torn apart. And all the knocking and the banging. I never heard the like of it. Wherever Paul is, I hope to God he wasn't out in it."

"Didn't I tell you he's up in Sweeney's or McAuley's? Jesus, he couldn't have been out in that, but knowing that fella I wouldn't put it past him." My mother glanced at him as if she was pleading.

"O Johnny, I just hope to God he's all right."

"For God's sake, didn't I tell you he's up with that bloody crowd. Sure they're probably still yammering away. They can't tell if it's morning or night. Too bloody busy listening to themselves. Did you ever watch that fella Sweeney going up and down the avenue? I'm sure he doesn't know where he is going half the time. Walks right past people. Say hello to him, and he looks at you as if you're mad. That bloody look stuck on his face. And that's the crowd that's going to change everything. Not a bloody day's work between them all, and they have all the answers."

My mother looked away from him and breathed deeply, and then she swallowed her tea. Her goitered throat shuddered as she swallowed, and her eyes stared. A long, bright beam of light fell across the kitchen floor.

My father finished his tea and reached his arms toward the ceiling, stretching.

"Well, I think I'll go for a ramble," he said. "Nothing like the air after a storm."

He moved to the hall and took his coat, and we heard the door close after him. Mary and my mother looked at each other, their eyes meeting, then Mary looked at me, not knowing what to say.

It was later that morning that we heard the front gate open and the slow steps on the path to the front door and then the knock. It was a sharp, frightening knock that was not familiar. My mother glanced at us, and I stood up to go to the door, but she pulled me back and went herself. I followed behind her, and when she opened the door I could see Mr. Fay, the policeman, standing there. He removed his hat and he said, "I wonder if I could come in for a minute, Mrs. Guiney." My mother nodded and stood aside and followed him into the kitchen. He was tall and red-faced, and I could see the mark of his hat across his forehead. There were dark purple veins in his cheeks, and he took out a handkerchief and blew his nose and then he looked at my mother and held his cap in his hands. She looked at him, bewildered and defiant at the same time. He turned his head toward the fire, then he looked at her again.

"I'm afraid I have some terrible news," he said. We all stared at him. "You better sit down, missus," he said to my mother, and she sat in her chair slowly and looked at him. Mary moved to her and stood by the side of the chair.

"We pulled Paul from the harbor this morning." He stopped and looked at us. "I'm afraid he had drowned, and there was nothing we could do." We stared at him and he looked at us and I refused to hear what he had told us. There was only the silence between us. We would stare at him forever and never hear what he said. My mother groaned and leaned forward until her head was touching her knees. Mary knelt beside the chair and put her arm around her shoulder and began to sob as she held my mother. Then my mother screamed and held her head up and her mouth was bared and the sound came from her throat. Her eyes were filled with tears, and I began to feel the pain that came over me. My stomach turned and my legs felt weak. It was as though they were gone and I couldn't feel myself standing. I knew he would die. I knew he wouldn't come back. I knew. I always knew there was no place for him, and even as the tears began to come from me, I was angry. So angry. I could see him laughing, staring at us with his mad smile. He was acting. He wasn't dead at all. For God's sake, Paul. Mary and my mother clung to each other, and Mr. Fay looked at me and didn't know what to say. He looked at them and he still held his hat in his hands and he turned to me again and said, "Run and get the woman next door." Just then there was a knocking on the door and I went to open it and Mrs. Cleary looked at me and ran into the kitchen and put her arms around Mary and my mother.

There were people outside the house. They knew. All the avenue knew and more people knocked on the door and came in. Outside they stared and talked softly among themselves. The children stood with them and looked in fear at the house.

"Paul Guiney drowned in the harbor," they whispered. "It was the storm. He was down by the sea and a wave came up and washed him away. Paul Guiney was mad. He was strange. He nearly drove his poor mother mad, too. Home from England for the Christmas. Oh, they change when they go there. Never the same when they come home. Left Guinness's. Best bloody job in Dublin. Left it. To go to England."

They spoke softly among themselves, and I knew what they were saying. They looked toward the house, and they nodded their heads. They moved aside when my father came. He walked into the house with his head down and his mouth set tightly, as if to hold something inside himself. I looked in through the kitchen door and he stood beside the three women and then he moved toward my mother. They stared at each other, not moving, and then he reached out and took her hand. His face didn't change. Then she turned away and stared at the floor. It was as though they were meeting for the first time and they didn't know what to say.

Mr. Fay still stood in the corner with his hat in his hands, and the women stood around my mother. My father turned away from them and looked at Mr. Fay and then he went over to him and they started to talk. Mr. Fay whispered.

"I don't know what it was, Johnny," he said. "They say he was on the pier and the storm at its worst. Two of the men say they saw him. They stopped and called out to him but he wouldn't budge. They couldn't go down onto the pier themselves, for fear of being washed away. They say he was holding onto the iron railing and the waves were breaking past him. Nobody could get near him. They say he must have had a drop taken. They say he was up in Silk's earlier in the day. He was laughing like a madman, they say, and then this morning they found him over by the yacht-club pier. There was nothing they could do, Johnny. He's in St. Michael's hospital now. You'll have to come down and identify him."

My father nodded and looked at his feet. His mouth was still set tightly. He seemed angry and looked around the kitchen. His lips moved as if he wanted to say something, but it wouldn't come, and when I could see his face I thought he would explode. I was afraid. His fists were clenched and he held them at his sides. As he looked around in desperation I thought he was going to shout, but then he turned back to Mr. Fay and placed a hand on his shoulder. His head was bowed and he sagged. Then he pulled himself up and shook his head slowly and began to cry.

I knew Paul was laughing, even as he lay in his coffin. Did he know something that made him laugh that way? Did he go straight to heaven? They didn't say where Paul was. "Bloody sad," they said. "Awful bloody thing, the way it happened." But I knew that he wasn't in heaven. He would always be laughing or arguing. He dismissed us.

Aunt Lill came home from England and Michael and Cissy came up from Gortmore. Even when they all sat in the living room talking and nodding their heads, I could feel him. I knew he was standing over their shoulders, laughing at them. Sometimes I had to hold the laughter back myself when I looked at them. All the nodding. All the shaking of the heads. All the long long talks that went on forever. All the sweet bewildered sadness.

There was a glory in it, too. We have been doing it for hundreds of years. Our fathers did it, and their fathers did it. We found this wonderful sadness under a bush. The same place we find our children. We were looking for something else, but we found this sadness. We better take it. Jesus, there must be some good in it. If we keep using it we'll get to the bottom of it. Time for sadness. Whipped by it. *Ochone. . . . Ochone. . . .* Oh, He's not a bad God. Not at all. He's all for the good, but be Jesus it's hard to tell sometimes. Shows us who's boss. Better not be too cocky now, because He's liable to do one of his tricks.

The crowds came to the house, all leaving a soft word. All to express the sorrow. All to show their amazement. Jesus it's hard to believe. He was the smartest one of them all. Oh, the brightest. It wouldn't do you to get into an argument with him. Oh, he'd pull you apart. The tongue of him. He stood up to everyone. Remember the way he put Mallon straight. Had them on their toes. He'd catch them. And politics. Never saw a fella could grasp a thing the way he could. It was more than that he had the facts of a thing. It was the savvy. Aye, the savvy. The things that came out of him. Sharp. And he knew it, too. In a way he was always apart from the rest of us. On his own. It was as though he couldn't wait for the rest of us to catch up to him. He changed, though. Aye, he did. He got so that he wouldn't talk to us. He'd have a jar with you. Give you the nod and the smile, but the talk was gone. He'd laugh. Ah politics me arse, he'd say. And we didn't see much of him since he came home.

Mallon came to the house, too, in the same black suit he always wore, with the thin white collar that said he was only a brother and not a priest. The little collar set him apart. Did he ever want to be a priest? Couldn't go the whole way. He spoke to my mother and father and he nodded to me. He put his hand on my shoulder.

"A terrible thing," he whispered. I watched him across the room, talking, his head nodding and his lips moving, the dark solemn look on his face.

Father Sheehan came, too, and spoke earnestly, his long white hair hanging over his forehead, nodding and whispering. In his element. Sure, isn't this what he's paid for? "Yes, yes, these things happen. They are a test for those that are left behind. There is no knowing the meaning. No knowing. We all must face it one day. All the while, though, all the while those of us who are here must go on. Isn't that it? We must go on in the face of all the madness. And the sadness." Mallon looked at him with his little half-collar, admiring the way the priest with the full collar did justice to his vocation.

The priest lifted his eyes to the crucifix on the wall and received the deep understanding of the death, then gave it to us. His lips moved and I could hear the low drone of his voice like an airplane high in the sky.

"Do not look for understanding. Ah, no. No. It is not God's business to give us the true understanding, because if we had it there would be no virtue in going on. Easy for St. Thomas. He saw. Did indeed. Stuck his hands in the wounds, healed though they were. Put his hands in them and then said My Lord and My God. But don't you see it was only after he had seen and felt."

I saw his lips moving afterward even as he ate the sandwich from the plate he held in his hand. They all looked at him. Even Sweeney and McAuley and Davin and Roe and the fellows who had worked with Paul in the brewery. There were people who said they drank with him in the pubs, but we didn't know them. They talked among themselves and nodded their heads and drank their bottles of porter. I wore a black armband and my father had a black tie. Mary and my mother were in black dresses. My mother's eyes were red all the time. There were times when she couldn't stand. She had to sit in the chair and dab at her eyes with the little white handkerchief she held between her fingers. Sometimes they all gazed aimlessly. The laughter rose when a story was told. Their eyes rose, their heads lifted, but still there was the fright in all of them. Each of them was alone, embarrassed as if they had been caught at something.

The sun shone down on the day of the funeral. We went to the church for the mass, and Father Sheehan wore his black vestments with the big gold cross on the back. Each time he turned to say "Dominus Vobiscum," I could see his face, and his lips were still moving as if stopping would let something in.

The coffin stood in the vestibule of the side entrance to the church, near the altar. There were two lighted candles at either end. The sun shone through the stained-glass windows of the vestibule, casting colored beams. I thought the lid would open at any minute and Paul would sit up and look around at us and laugh. I could see him pointing at the priest when he turned to give the blessing, and when he came to the coffin with the holy water and splashed it, Paul ducked and held his hands up so he wouldn't get wet. As the pallbearers carried the coffin down the aisle, he sat on the top of it and he had a peashooter and was blazing away at them. When they carried him out of the church into the brightness of the day he stood up and saluted, and then he started to sing. All the way to the cemetery he sat on the coffin, looking back at us as we followed him. He pointed at Sweeney and McAuley and Davin and Roe and he looked at Mallon and shook his head. The procession went up Sutton's Hill and passed by the field and the Boley Woods. The same trees were still tall and dark and silent as we passed. I thought about the hut, and I knew I could never go into it again.

At the top of the hill we could see the purple mountains. The old mountains. They rose up to the sky and the sun sparkled on them. I looked back down the hill at all the cabs behind us. So many people we didn't know.

"A lot of the crowd here he drank with," my father said. "Don't know them at all." And when we arrived at the cemetery there was a crowd waiting for us. All the people I knew from the town. The little man on the wheels and the woman we thought was the Virgin Mary and Nicholas

Ryan stood under a tree looking at the crowd and holding onto his bicycle. I saw all the people who walked the roads during Davy's inquest. They all came and they looked.

I could see the headstones, row after row of them standing silently in the sun. Each one solitary. All the names and the dates—soon they would reach all the way to the mountains. All the sad crosses. And there were angels with opened wings and benign faces looking like death. The dark, black hole waited for the coffin and the crowd stood looking at Father Sheehan as he read the prayers. We were in a circle around the hole and I stood with my mother and father and Mary. My grandfather held my mother's arm and my father stood on the other side of her. Aunt Lill and Mary were behind her and she stared at the hole. Dorry McQueen stood opposite me and when she stared I kept my eyes on her as the wind blew her hair. Mrs. McQueen looked fierce. The awful angry look on her face, furious that such a thing could happen again. Bloody madness the whole thing. She chewed her little piece of seaweed and she looked at Father Sheehan as if she didn't believe a word he said.

The wind blew gently and the soft white clouds passed by. I always still looked for the one with the star on its tail but I never saw it. Would it ever come across the sky again? Father Sheehan shook the holy water onto the coffin, and I could see the drops glisten. Then the grave diggers came in their mud-covered boots, and they began to lower it into the hole. And still Paul was sitting on the outside looking at them, enjoying the journey to the bottom. They began to shovel the clay down on top of it. He laughed and ducked. But they didn't stop.

I sat beside Mary on the way home and my head fell on her shoulder. I could feel her softness against me, and then she leaned toward me. I was so tired. All the tears were gone. There was only the tiredness that made me numb. I wanted to stay in the cab and keep going on forever. I didn't want to go home. Just let the cab go on and on and we won't even look out the window. We'll pull the shades down, and we'll pass through the world, and we'll never know where we are.

One day after the funeral Dorry came to the house for me and we went walking to Killiney Hill. We looked out over the bay and I saw the place I loved and how it frightened me. We could see down toward the Wicklow Mountains with the purple haze covering them and the water sparkling in the bay. It was beautiful and sad, and I was pulled and held. The world was so beautiful and so frightening, the way it looked at me and asked me questions. It brought me to it, and it pushed me away. It held me, and it let me go. It asked me nothing, and it asked me everything. It listened to me, and it turned on me, and it could fill me with the deepest fear.

The deep green grass was all around us, and the sky was blue. The deep ancient grass. Dorry lay with me that day and held me to her. I could feel her through her dress, soft and full, holding me. I could feel her breasts as she kissed my neck and I felt the warmth of her. Her smell. I could feel her around me. Enclosing me. So gentle, so full of the ancient tenderness. She was joined to all things and all time. Children always. Children of all time. And still, even as she lay with me, Paul's death was only a rumor. But the rumor would never go away. They had called to him on the pier in the midst of the storm, but he wouldn't come back. Rumors. It was as though life was a rumor, too. Dorry was real. Everything else is a rumor. We have heard there is a lifting and a joy. We have heard there is salvation. We have heard there will be a time when we will all have jobs. We have heard of London. There is a story, they say, called *Hamlet*. Paul had a copy. A red-covered copy. He carried it with him. We have heard that he was brilliant. We have heard that he died. Life is full of things I only hear, and then it is upon me. It arrives and it is still only a rumor. A shadow that passes by and tells me it is life. A rumor.

I believed Guinness's had gone away, that there would never be a letter. They had forgotten I had ever been there. But then one morning when I was still half-asleep the bedroom door opened and my mother appeared with the open letter in her hand.

"You didn't get it, Jackie," she said very softly. I looked at her face and her lips were quivering. Her eyes were moist and she was weary.

"I'm sorry," I said. My mouth was dry and I couldn't swallow. The sorrow was only for her, and she said, "Never mind, you did your best. It's been here since before Christmas but I thought we could have the Christmas one way or the other and not be bothered by what the letter had to say."

She looked at me and put the letter in her apron pocket,

and then she turned and went down the stairs to the kitchen. I could hear her putting the teacups on the table, and I heard the pot scraping the stove and the sound of the tea being poured. Through the window I could hear the sound of the Clearys next door. They were fighting again. I heard the yells and the curses and the children crying. It subsided and a door slammed and steps hurried down the lane.

I went to Sutton's Field that day and wore my new football boots. I ran and ran and never stopped. I leaped so high I could feel myself rising up to the sky. I felt the boots on my feet and looked at them as I ran. When I sat the sweat rolled down my face and I looked up not knowing, still knowing all.

If something doesn't go one way, it will go another, my mother used to say. There is magic. The trees do dance in the Boley Woods at night when there is no one looking. Paul isn't dead, he is with me all the time, and Guinness's made a mistake. My father will let me go to work with him. He will show me to all the men. They will smile at me. There is magic. Johnny Seery said no one believes in it anymore.

"Believe and they laugh at you," he said, "and chase you down the roads. And sure, what is it, only feeling. They don't know that. Aye, they never know what they feel. All the years of looking down from the balcony. The fathers and the sons and the mothers and the daughters. The men afraid to know tenderness, and the women afraid to give it. The strain I see on the faces. All holding back, and the auld place looking at them, as sad as they are. I've often said they should build a fierce fire in the middle aisle. Aye, and throw all the books of history into it, aye, and watch the flames roar up and out to the sky. And the saints and the patriots and the heroes would all go floating up with them. We'd be shut of them. Sure Jasus, we could never tell which way is up anyway.

How could we with the incense and the piety and the heads looking at the floor? And me up in the balcony, pumping the auld organ. Aye, indeed, you might well ask, auld son, which way is up."

I had a madness. Paul left it to me, and when it was my time to leave I took it with me. I had it, yes, but still I knew there was something. There was a place in me I knew was there and it would see me through my madness. The madness of my innocence. Aunt Jenny wrote that she would take me to America.

"Are you going to go then?" my father asked me. I could only nod to him. He nodded, too, and turned away from me. What else is there to do? I saw Joe Kavanaugh through the window at the bus stop as he waited to go to the brewery, and Maguire passed with the others on their way to the secondary in their scarves and their blazers. They had their places and now I would have mine. I gave my football away when I knew I was going to leave. My lovely black boots. My mother brought me to Dublin and bought me new underwear and a suitcase. I lost her in the crowds that day, when we walked on Henry Street. I searched up and down the streets for her and I ached for her and Dublin was still so gray. I didn't want to go but I could never tell them. I was going to leave them all behind. It was a rumor and an expectation and salvation for failure. We had all died so long ago.

On the morning I was leaving, my father came to my bed before he went to work and sat on the edge. He put his hand on my shoulder.

"Good-bye, son," he said. "Watch yourself. Write to your mother. God bless." It wasn't light yet and I couldn't see his face. Then he moved away and went down the stairs. I heard the gate clang after him and I heard his footsteps on the road and he was gone. I lay awake in the room. All the nights I had waited. The room of all my fear and all of my enchantments. The darkness began to leave and the light came silently and my mother knocked on my door. She was beautiful and warm and I thought of the mornings she had sat me on the kitchen table. Her smell. I asked her not to cry.

"Oh, don't cry," I said, but she did, and she tried to smile. I wouldn't cry.

My mother stood at the door of the house and waved till I was gone. Her sad, anxious look. Her fear and her bewilderment standing at the door with her. It was like another death. I was ashamed.

When the ship pulled away from Cobh I stood at the rail and looked back. The land reaching down to the sea, beckoning, calling me back. The shadowy misty land lying there like a wounded dog with its legs reaching out into the sea. All those who had gone before me. They all saw the same thing. I felt so small and alone, standing at the rail. So hard to look back. So full of failure. I could see them sitting in the kitchen. I knew how sad they were. Someday we will all know each other. I could hardly see the land now. I looked back through the mist. There was only a dark shadow. Almost gone. Time to turn away.

I walked toward the bow, and the old song came through me. The song I always heard and I could see the vast sea ahead.